The Question
She Put To Herself

The Question She Put To Herself

Stories by Maureen Brady

The Crossing Press/Freedom, California 95019
The Crossing Press Feminist Series

PS
3552
.R2435
Q4
1987

Cover photograph by Ron Wu

Typeset by *The Ithaca Times*
   in English Times 10/12

Printed in the U.S.A.

My thanks go to Sandy Boucher, Pearl Mindell, Linda Smuckler, and Susanna Sturgis for support in the making of this book, and/or for their responses to some of the stories, and most especially to Cheryl Moch, for both. Thanks also to Kate Dunn and Elaine Goldman Gill of The Crossing Press for their efforts in publishing it.

I am gratefully indebted to The McDowell Colony, The Cummington Community for the Arts, Briarcombe, and The Millay Colony for the Arts for the precious time in which many of these stories were written.

Preface

These stories span the past dozen years, 1975-1986, a time of enormous change as I saw it, both in the exterior world and within my interior.

"'Chiggers,'" "Grinning Underneath," "The Question She Put to Herself," and "On the Way to the ERA," emerged in a climate of intense feminist activity (1975-77). In fact, "On the Way to the ERA" should be dedicated to the women's political study group to which I belonged for several years, since it was my response to our discussion of the topic — reform versus revolution.

"Novena" was written in 1978. "The Field Is Full of Daisies . . . ," written in 1981 and '82, is an autobiographical account of an accident I experienced in 1978.

"Strike It Rich" was written in 1982-83, in dedication to my father, Francis J. Brady, 1908-1981, who was both a fine oral storyteller and a quiz show contestant.

"Seneca Morning," "Early Autumn Exchange," "Care in the Holding," and "Corsage" were all written in the period from 1983-86. "Seneca Morning" is dedicated to my inspired and inspiring friend, Barbara Deming (1917-1984), who was there, and who yet resides close in her spirit.

December, 1986
West Hurley, N.Y.
Maureen Brady

Contents

Strike It Rich

ME and my brother and sister sit about three feet from the brand new twenty-one inch T.V. Our baby brother, Dewey, toddles up and down the room on the thatched rug which is the only protection from the cool, hard tile of the floor should he stumble and fall and bump his head. We have just moved to Florida and this is the first T.V. we have ever had. When we lived up north on the chicken farm only our rich neighbors had one, and seeing it required conniving a reason to get into their house, then sidling into the living room where it occupied center stage. I would feel like a burglar stealing into that room, but Mary would push me ahead, saying, "Lee Ann, we're just going to look 'n see what's on T.V." Mostly it was snow until they got hooked up to the antenna on the hill, but we would watch until we got good and bored. Often it was snowing outside, too, and when we'd saturate with boredom, we'd go back out to the real stuff.

It is eleven-thirty on a summer morning. The jalousie windows are open but there isn't much of a breeze. When it does blow, it stirs up the smell of freshly poured cement. The memory is beginning to fade, but only a short time ago we lived in the Royal Palms Motel and drove to this Citrus Estates subdivision every couple of days to survey the progress on the house. We'd

1

stare at the concrete block walls which had been erected abruptly in our absence and realize — wow, this is my room, or — hey, this room is the biggest — is it the living room or the master bedroom? We'd tear about with our confusion. The fact that the floor plans said *master* bedroom; the fact that the neighborhood was called Citrus *Estates*; the fact that our parents tried never to talk about money in front of us children: these facts sat on top of question marks in our nimble, pre-television brains. We knew we weren't rich; we knew this couldn't be an *estate*. We knew we had moved because of money, because our father was going back to sea, where he had come from before the farm, and where he had gone when he was fifteen and his father died and he'd stepped into the role of provider.

We knew without being told that this was mother's house. She'd said, "If *you're* going back to sea, *I'm* going where it's warm," and then she got the map out and showed us all where Florida was, and that turned into wouldn't you like to go there? No, no, no, no, no, I'd hollered inside. All my friends, my room, my house, my barns, my hills, my berry patch, my apple orchard, all settled around me, all woven through me, part of me. I saw myself hiding in the attic of the house across the street, looking out the dormer window onto our house, adoring it — the huge maples that stood so tall in the front yard, the wide sweep of the side porch, which was where we set up rainy day games of Monopoly. From there, I imagined myself watching the family drive away without me, the little two tone green Nash Rambler station wagon that didn't have room for all of us anyway, loaded down heavy in the back, climbing the hill and taking the last curve out of town. In this way I avoided thinking about actually having to move right up to the very last moment, when I was assigned the middle of the back seat, as befit my role as second child, and was packed in along with everything else we had chosen to keep out of the auction.

The fact of the Florida house going up surely meant we weren't tourists. We weren't rich either, but I'd thought only rich people built new houses. There was a sign out front we always had to pass — NO TRESPASSING — DO NOT ENTER — and the whole time we wandered around those hollow walls, I feared being caught trespassing, never called out to the others but whispered, and often they answered in whispers.

We'd look up to the sky and see the stars and giggle at the idea you could see stars from *inside* a house. For me, I wouldn't have minded leaving it that way. It was warm like Mommy wanted. Imagine standing out at night in shorts and the breeze cooled you by its motion, not by bringing in the north wind. It was consoling to think she must be happy with this. No, I did not want or need a roof on this house. Boring as it was at the Royal Palms Motel, change was coming too fast.

"Next time we come the roof'll be on," Daddy said.

No, I didn't believe it. There were only four carpenters and the construction of a roof seemed an enormous task. We couldn't go and watch them build during the daytime because Daddy went to Unemployment or else was off following up leads, thinking he might find a stay-home job, though we all knew he was going back to sea as soon as he got us situated in the new house. The next day, everywhere I looked I saw ants building ant hills. I wanted them to stop, to rest, but they went on relentlessly, pushing one grain of sand to the top, returning for another. I had to sit on my feet to hold back from flattening the hills with one simple swipe of my big toe.

Sure enough when we returned, the roof was on, settling like doom between us and the stars, but at least the breeze still blew through the holes that were meant for windows. Mom couldn't wait for the house to be finished. She walked around with hungry, decorator eyes, thinking out loud about colors, arrangement of the furniture we didn't have, starting fresh. "Isn't it nice to start fresh," she'd say, her voice light and airy with bright ideas. Mary, twelve and adventuresome, would agree. I'd say *sort of* even though it had wrecked the first ten years of my life, and terrible Timothy, the grouch, nine, would give her a mean look. Dewey would be toddling around, testing echoes with his screeches in the various rooms, or spilling out huge boxes of sevenpenny nails on the floor. Mommy, surviving inside her frilly fantasies, decided to paint the outside of the house pink. Coral, she called it, and that word built in the imagination, but when it came off the paint brushes onto the

3

concrete blocks, it was just plain pink.

Mary and Timmy and me are sitting all hunched up close, both to each other and to the new T.V. in the new house, on the "grass" rug, which leaves markings all over your bare legs if you so much as watch one whole program without moving around. The NO TRESPASSING sign is down and we are now actual residents of Citrus Estates, though it is still hard to believe this is home the way our farmhouse was. Our farmhouse had a woolly rug in the room we played in and drapes heavy enough to hide behind on all the windows. This place seems more like a cross between our real home and the Royal Palms Motel.

Mary and I have a room together like we did before, and Timmy and Dewey have a room with bunkbeds. Mommy and Daddy have the master bedroom but Daddy has gone back to sea so Mommy has it all to herself (really more space than she needs). Daddy has not yet found a job to take him far out on the ocean, but he works on tug boats in New York Harbor for two weeks at a time, then has one week off. We can't afford for him to come home since we live so far away, (in this place that may one day blow away in a hurricane), so on his week off he goes around trying to get on quiz shows and we stay home, watching for him.

We are watching "Strike It Rich" and we know this is one he has tried for and then Warren Hull is saying, "Our next contestant, Mr. Franklin Sperry," and Daddy is there, flat figure on our screen in the Coral house and we are all calling, "Mommy, come quick, Daddy is on T.V." Dewey comes with his greasy fingers and touches Daddy on the picture tube and Mary lunges on him and pulls him into her lap to watch. Mom stops sweeping the sand, which she claims enters this house as if each of us shoveled the beach into our shoes. She comes and stands behind our backs, propped against the broom. I think she is even more amazed than we are to see Daddy like this. I can't hear anyone breathing. It is like he is watching us, watching our existence in the Coral house, instead of us watching him. His face is broad, as it is in real life, and his look is direct. He smiles for a second, which we take as a message for us, then Warren Hull asks him would he please tell the viewers his story.

4

I am suddenly, rigidly aware that this is not all a game, that for weeks now we have been listening to the sad stories of the contestants on this program. I have often been quietly moved to tears by them. I have known that telling why you are poor or unfortunate is a requirement for getting on the program, but I have never thought to put this together with a picture of my dad, standing there like he is now, shifting his body slightly inside the suit which I've only ever seen him wear to church. He's saying — my wife, she was a city girl . . . I met her on a cruise on a ship I was sailing then . . . we went up country together . . . hard adjustment for her but she was willing . . . worked hard, both worked hard trying to make it with a small chicken farm . . . no big equipment . . . just the family . . . children worked too, as soon as they were old enough . . . (How fast I'd forgotten the chores — gather eggs, grade eggs, pack eggs, feed my own little bantam hens I was raising for a 4-H project. Life so simple in the pink house, squeezing grapefruit and watching T.V.) . . . bankruptcy . . . give up on the farm . . . go back to sea. Family's in Florida now . . . trying to get back on our feet.

I am crying now the way I do when I am moved by other people's stories on Strike It Rich; the tears rise to my eyes and stay on the edges of them until they evaporate. The word bankruptcy has stuck inside me, making me feel as if a boat has overturned in my stomach. I don't know what the word means but I am riveted to it as a key to my confusion. Does it mean the bank has something to do with our lives? One reason it is hard to figure this is that we didn't even have a bank in our town. Despite the fact that I feel sick, I maintain an appearance of calm but avid interest in this T.V. program, and I suspect I'm not the only one. I don't dare look to see how anyone else is reacting because I can feel that shock has made us all into statues, still and silent to anyone but ourselves. Mom is propped on the broom, her bare arms sticking out of her sleeveless blouse, her bare legs sticking out of her bermuda shorts. We are all very exposed. We have come here to start over, but Daddy is on T.V. in living rooms all over the country and, perhaps more to the point, all over Citrus Estates.

I can see that he would like to loosen his tie. He always does that as soon as he exits from the church, pulls his tie first one way, then the next, then releases the top button of his shirt and sighs, as if he had only been getting a limited supply of air through the bottleneck of his throat surrounded by the stiff collar, the noose of the tie.

His story is finished. Dewey is clapping for Daddy, the audience is clapping, Mommy shifts her relationship to the broom and begins to clap and then we all do. The sounds of our claps ring on the concrete walls, the stark floor. We do not have *enough* in this house yet to be clapping, singing, laughing, shouting. We have a cheap sofa with bolsters, a grass rug, a picture of a lone seagull on the wall. We have a father who comes to us on T.V., working for his honor, telling us about a family we barely recognize.

They have cut to a Fab commercial but we do not cut our attention from the screen except to release Dewey for thirty seconds of toddling. We all stare silently at the woman examining her wash for whiteness and Mommy hums the jingle without seeming to know she is doing so.

Now back to Daddy and we are ready to play Strike It Rich except while the camera comes in on Daddy, Warren Hull summarizes his story for anyone who tuned in during the commercial. I hope that he will explain bankruptcy, but of course he doesn't. As the words come out of his mouth, our story becomes a public story. It belongs to the show now, which is fine with me — they can have it. "Come on, come on, let's play the game," Timmy mutters to Warren. The camera is on both of them now, and I like the way Warren looks, so friendly to Daddy and yet so comfortable in his suit.

There are categories such as history, music, sports, famous figures, and sometimes Daddy gets to choose the category, sometimes not. After the category is chosen, he decides how much to put on the question, and the more money he goes for, the harder the question he draws. He starts out slow and easy and he's doing fine. He gets all the answers. He lets go of a little grin after each one, then I can see how his concentration is moving forward to be ready for the next. This is how he was also when he was home with us, after we got the T.V. He would sit on

6

the sofa, trunk bent forward, elbows on his knees, and volunteer the answers to the contestants before they responded. Chuckling lightly when they missed. A big $400 is lit up on the screen. This is what he is winning so far, we are winning so far. We are already spending it, at least I am, and I suspect I am not alone. It feels as if we are all one person at this moment, though I know we will argue later about how we would each spend it if it were our own. I would try to begin to fill up the pink house more.

Warren Hull is saying, "Do you understand?" and Daddy bobs his head. What is to be understood is that he has just put double or nothing on the last question and he does not get to choose the category. If he answers correctly, we will win $800. If he does not, we will lose the $400. We hold our breath. It is unbelievable that our life might change so fast.

I grab Mary's hand and we both squeeze hard. I just know he is going to lose and wish he had gotten on The Price Is Right instead. That is his favorite quiz show and I know he could win on it. He knows exactly how much everything costs. He knows the difference between the price of a Sears refrigerator and a Montgomery Wards. He knows stoves, he knows cars, toasters, irons, washing machines. His hobby is pricing things. While other people go shopping to buy, he goes around memorizing price tags. He comes home and reports to us and tells us his ideas about why Wards is charging more. He knows motors, too, so he knows they have identical motors, these refrigerators. He wants to understand the psychology of pricing, but he doesn't. He believes no one should charge more than is absolutely necessary. Mom says there are hundreds of reasons why prices might come out different, but he doesn't believe her. He doesn't even ask her what they are and she doesn't tell, so I don't know what to think. Just like with the eggs I didn't know what to think. All the time they used to talk about the egg prices up, the egg prices down — way down sometimes — Daddy frowning, his bushy eyebrows nearly coming to meet. It didn't seem fair that if the hens had a good laying season the egg prices should drop. We'd be working harder and so would the hens. Why then should everyone else be going around rejoicing about cheap eggs? Daddy tried to explain the balance, the system of supply and demand, but I wasn't ever convinced that he bought it. An egg was an egg where we were concerned.

They flash $800 in a light bulb design off and on the screen. This isn't because he has won it already, but to tell how excited we are that he might. Warren Hull's low voice has risen to a higher pitch as if he wants us to win it, and I hope this means he has a way of pulling an easy question for the last one. Mary slips her legs under her, comes up to kneeling, and whispers, "Come on, Daddy, you can do it."

Now the category comes jumping out — MUSIC — and Mom sighs, *oh, no*, and we all droop. Still rapt but we can no longer think of spending the eight hundred. Daddy is tone deaf. He can't sing. He doesn't listen when we do or even when music is played. He reads a paper or watches out the window or goes off in his own mind playing with the prices. This is awful. We try to sink slowly but Mary sinks the fastest because of kneeling. I have just filled up the house with eight hundred dollars worth of stuff and they are playing a song, something familiar but I wouldn't know what to name it myself. I say, *come on, come on, please, Daddy*, over and over inside. *You've probably heard the name of it somewhere. Just relax and let the answer come to you.* His eyes are looking around as if time is taking too long to pass, and I can see he has no where more to search for the answer. They only played the first few bars. Now those bars are fading in my memory and in the silence I could make them into almost any song, then venture a guess, but he doesn't even do that. "I don't know," he says, shrugging the weight of his shoulders which are abnormally squared off from the shoulder pads in his suit.

"What is it?" I whisper to Mommy.

"The Blue Danube Waltz," she says, mouthing the title to Daddy, but she knows, we all know, that he will never get it. Timmy is beating his legs with his fists. "I'll give you one more chance," Warren says, and replays the same bars of music. But this is only making it worse. Making us wait and wait, making Daddy shift uncomfortably foot to foot, his eyes losing their sparkle. I am chanting to myself — blue danube waltz blue danube waltz. We know it is lost but we are still trying. Now would be a good time for the hurricane to come and blow us away. Daddy is beginning to look stupid, which finally, is worse than bankruptcy. They ring a bell that means time is up and they erase the light board that was holding our money. At least we can breathe.

"Too bad," Warren says. "Bad luck for our contestant." But now the heartline lights up. This is a telephone with lights all around it and as the phone rings, the lights flash, pumping my adrenalin back up so my heart is a knot. Warren's voice is calm enough to make me think the world will go on, no matter what, as he says, "Well, let's see who's calling." He listens and then conveys the message. The caller is an ex-actor from New York City who moved upstate to try his hand at chicken farming and has been quite successful, so he's donating seventy-five dollars to help Franklin Sperry and his family get back on their feet. "How nice of him," Mommy says. I don't think it's nice at all. How come he was able to succeed? And what will a mere seventy-five dollars be able to buy? I don't want to have to be grateful to this stranger. I don't want to have people all over the country, sitting in their living rooms, saying, "How nice, aren't they lucky this man decided to give them some money." If Daddy had won, that would have been something else. Or if the man was willing to donate eight hundred dollars, I'd be willing to say thanks.

Daddy is gone now. He is off the air and a new contestant is telling her story, but we don't follow her. It seems very pale to watch a stranger on T.V.

Timmy curses and Mommy scolds him for it, but he goes on anyway, a grin loping across his face. "Quite a sob story he told, wasn't it?" Dewey is first to giggle at this, then at me. I say, "Yeah, he really laid it on." I wait for Mommy to say, "No, that was real, that was us he was talking about," but she doesn't. She starts to hum "The Blue Danube Waltz," goes on beyond those first few bars they played, letting the hum swell louder as she goes. We are all a mass of giggles now. Mary rolls off her knees over onto her side, her pretty face away from me, but I hear her join in, saying, "He laid it on pretty thick." I tickle Dewey, then Mary tickles me, then she turns on Timmy.

He tries to hold a straight face, to resist feeling. His brown hair waves at the same place on his forehead as Daddy's hair does. He looks like Daddy did when he was waiting out the time. Then tiny little spits fly out of his mouth as he breaks into laughter. This seems very, very funny.

"You're spitting at me, can't you control your spit?" Mary says, as she keeps on tickling him. "Can't control your spit, can you?" She turns back to me. "How about you?" I get serious, hold my breath. Think numb and try not to feel her fingers digging along my ribs except as nuisances, but I hear Mommy still humming the tune. She's gone back in the kitchen with the broom and is sweeping and humming, and my throat is filling and I burst, rocking on the grass rug with my laughter that's hurting my stomach and my face.

Still somewhere in the far back reach of my mind, I am doing fractions, which we've been studying at school, and trying to figure out what fraction of $12,000 is $800. Because I think it is $12,000 we are paying for this pink house over the next twenty years. It might be $12,500 because we got a corner lot. We are all rolling and rocking and spitting out our laughter and Dewey keeps running, leaping and then falling onto our mass of bodies, and I don't know how we'll ever be able to stop.

"Stop," I gasp. "We've got to stop."

"Can't," Mary spits out.

We've got to ask *what's bankruptcy,* I'm thinking, feeling the indentations on the backs of my legs from the grass rug as if they were symptoms of some big disease. I can't ask it. Instead, I say, "Maybe tomorrow he'll get on The Price Is Right."

"Yeah," Timmy says, his laughter dying to contempt. "They don't have any *music* on that one."

I wonder when will Mommy be able to have a piano again. It's the one thing I don't think Daddy has priced. But I've never seen them give one away on The Price Is Right anyway. I'm thinking how it's hard to imagine where we would put it in this hollow sounding room so that its notes wouldn't just echo off the walls. Then I realize the house is different now. It does not seem so empty or so new as it bounces our laughter back at us.

Early Autumn Exchange

A grand sugar maple stands in the front yard out near the road. Lauren has arranged her desk at the window so she looks directly at this tree. She imagines its roots curling and snarling deep down to bedrock. She grew up with such trees which may be why staring at this one makes her feel more at home in her new farmhouse apartment than anything else she has yet found there. Two women, longer armed than she, could stand on either side of the trunk and reach around and touch fingertips — just that, no more. It is early September and the tree is full as can be with green. There is another down the pasture line which has a burst of red along its side, but this one holds the rich end of summer in suspension and will probably be last to turn and shed its leaves.

Lauren is short and sturdy. She wonders how much is she molded by the idea that she should *be* as she *appears*? Because right now she does not feel sturdy. Her eyes trace the roots where they snake out from the trunk to where they take their course underground only a few feet away. She wishes she could see them go further.

Her mother calls out from Lauren's kitchen, "Shall I baste the chicken?" and Lauren calls back, "Sure, go ahead." Though her voice sounds casual, she is frenzied by the pair of urges which arise from this simple question — the desire to do absolutely everything for herself, opposing her desire to turn back to infancy and let her mother do everything. Surely there is some middle ground but she does not know where to find it, or when she does, how to be peaceful with it. Lauren reasons with herself: you did, after all, fix the chicken the way you like it and put it in the oven, so you are not letting your mother do it all. It's not Lauren's style to hang out with cooking. When she is alone, she sets the timer to remind herself the food is prepared and needs to be eaten when it's done.

This will be the last supper with her mother for a while. Her mother will be going to Chapel Hill in the morning, to visit her niece, who's just had a baby, a creature which gives Madeline a fortifying role, surrogate grandmother. Lauren creates art, a harder thing to grandmother. She is forty and does not expect to have children. She has been a lesbian for a decade and has told her mother it would be good to accept this, since she does not plan to change it. She plans to live alone now, with this tree out there grounding her. Before this she lived six years with her lover in a spacious old house, nested in a hollow between hills.

Lauren draws herself reluctantly from the tree and goes to put up water for the corn. While her new kitchen has more cupboards than she's used to, the counters are cluttered with her unpacked boxes because she's trying to rid the place of roaches before putting away her things. The roach battle is a royal annoyance when her real fight is so clearly elsewhere, with her ex. The kitchen walls are lemon yellow, too bright. The color sets off bitter squirts in Lauren's salivary glands. Either her body will adapt or she'll have to cover these walls with a more neutral color.

She gets out place mats, and standing sturdy, holding them to her chest, stares at the table. Where shall she sit? Where shall she place her mother? These place mats, burnt orange with floral napkins to match were a gift from her sister last Christmas, and she is grateful for them. So many things had to be split between her and Bess. Their origin had to be remembered — did they buy them together or who gave them and to whom? While her family had not known she was thinking of leaving all that year, strangely, even her rarely-gives-gifts-sister had sent her pot holders and bread pans for her birthday.

Finally Lauren chooses the chair facing the window for herself and sets her mother at the opposite place. Always she takes much of her orientation from seeing outdoors, and now, reeling from the loss of her home, from the strangeness of the sound of this old-but-new-to-her refrigerator, from the temptation to turn back to infancy, she needs to at least see out.

Madeline, widowed two years now, has a luster in her eyes that speaks of new self assurance. Lauren wants to address that luster but doubts her mother would be able to own it. She suspects her mother feels safer when she is burdened by her grief. She knows that *she* does — that she hardly dares to speak of her relief at being free of Bess. If she were to shine with it, what then? She fears punishment. Her community is made up of brave, rule-breaking dykes who, despite their liberationist stance, don't like to see anyone liberated at the expense of anyone else. They listen for the cues of who is most victimized. Lauren wonders is this the case, also, in her mother's widow's circle, or do they allow the births that come out of grief to shine through?

She remembers what happened to her mother at the annual church auction which took place a week after Lauren's father had died. Though still in shock, Madeline, who had collected many of the items, decided to participate as previously planned. The auctioneer droned: "Ladies and Gentlemen . . . available next . . . look what we have . . ." as she brought forth the objects for sale. On her last trip forward, she carried a lamp, and holding it high, declared, "This is a lovely lamp." Then, without warning, her mouth had gone on moving, the words had come out — "I'm available, too." Her hand had jumped reflexively to cover her mouth. Her face had reddened and she'd turned away. "I don't know if I'll ever be able to face the neighbors again," she'd told Lauren. An old and familiar refrain. Madeline always projected on her neighbors. Lauren felt self-righteous because she didn't care about her neighbors, but, if she wanted to be honest, she had to admit she projected on her community, and even when she could see what she was doing, she couldn't stop, because it was the only way she had of getting a feeling outside herself.

They are halfway through a dinner which has thus far held more silence than either of them is normally capable of sustaining, when Madeline clears her throat to speak. "Do you think there's still a chance for reconciliation?" It takes Lauren a second to focus, to realize the question is about her and Bess. She was not feeling the loss just then. She was distracted by the sweetness of the fresh corn and had been sucking the sugar from the cob and savoring its taste.

"I guess so," she says, "but not right now, at least not living together."

Madeline eats the corn neatly. She begins a row at the larger end, then follows through on what she has started, her teeth carefully closing over only the kernels that fall in the right lines. Her teeth are straight. Lauren is grateful Madeline is busy with the corn instead of chattering, which she has a tendency to do when nervous. Thin, white hair frames the sharp bones of her face. Lauren studies how the corners of her mother's lips are straight and searches her memory for the old angle she thinks they used to hold. Has widowhood let the tension out of those muscles that always pulled her mouth ever so slightly down? While the lines in her face have the depth of her seventy years in them, there is a strong sense of change in her mother, more than Lauren has seen in years. She is almost sure of it, yet it is hard to distinguish this from the shifting and moving in herself, the early autumn change. Might she not be reflecting herself onto her mother? The wrinkles of Madeline's forehead and brow always seemed to hold a look of bafflement. Might that have come to seem like a mask, the wrong look for her feeling?

Lauren wants to explain more about her and Bess, but she hasn't been able to explain to herself. Still, she tries. "When I change . . . when I don't do what she wants me to do, I don't think she likes me. She makes excuses for me. Like the last time we tried to talk and I disagreed with her about everything that came up, she said, 'I know you're upset because you lost your cat.' I *was* upset about my cat, but I also disagreed with her." Lauren sighs. She feels so far from any statement that could

14

possibly summarize her feelings. Her stomach heaves with the trying. "I let her harbor the idea I would drop out and give in to what she wanted, rather than raise a conflict. And after a while I didn't even know what I wanted." A hunger wells inside her as she says this; it is the empty place filled with sadness, where she has missed herself. Holding back tears, she goes to the stove for another ear of corn, and offers one to her mother.

"Yes, they're delicious," Madeline says.

"I couldn't go back unless there was really room for two whole people." Lauren hesitates, then adds, "And I was sure I could keep myself one of them."

Her mother butters the corn, then looks up at her. "Maybe you're not meant to be with somebody." Lauren flinches and her deep blue eyes, which are the eyes of her father, squint. She gazes out on the pasture, the board fence of the paddock her landlady rents out in summer. The paddock is barren now, recovering from the hard use of the recently departed horses. She feels banished and has no retort. "I meant," her mother continues, "there was a whole line of people in your father's family who never married or centered their lives around a relationship."

Lauren is alarmed at how much has jangled off in her; how much she knows, yet how hard it is to keep from going underground with her feelings. She has heard the twang in her mother's attitude and knows it is not just hermitude she is talking about, but lesbianism, the idea that it derives from *his* side of the family. This notion has come up before and Lauren had thought she had countered it successfully, but now she sees it was only stuffed in Madeline's closet. She wonders: is it possible to speak with emphasis but without screaming and somehow finds the courage to try. "Mother, I *have* just spent the past seven years of my life in a serious relationship."

"I know," Madeline says. "I was thinking about the future."

Lauren is pierced by a sudden flash of her mother's perspective that a lesbian without a lover is less of a lesbian than a lesbian with a lover. The presence of the corn seems to help her hold her eye on this view. Without looking away from Madeline, she nibbles down the last row and begins sucking the sweet juice from the cob again. One part of her remains there with her mother, while the rest of her departs into fantasy, where she imagines her mouth fitting nicely over the soft breast of another woman. She feels how her sucking pulls at the breast *and* pulls inside her like a tide which makes her belly begin to tighten and tingle. Her mother's voice she hears as if it comes from the other end of a tunnel. The words are those that came at the restaurant in Florida, last time they talked about *the subject.*

"You know, there's only one thing that still bothers me about your lesbianism."

"What's that?" Lauren had asked, feigning normal breathing.

Madeline had glanced sideways to gauge the distance of the neighboring tables, then the corners of her mouth drawn in tight, she'd said, "The sexual part. I just stop there and can't imagine . . ."

"I don't really expect you to," Lauren had said, "I don't sit around imagining you having sex to accept you as a hetero-sexual person."

But now she does. She tries to picture how sex was for her mother with her father. Was it a place of wonder? A battle-ground? Did she get what she wanted? Did she hold back when she was angry, which was nearly always, though rarely ex-pressed? Was she always on her back or did she sometimes go on top of his larger body? Lauren remembers the muffled sounds of their sex coming through the bedroom wall, remembers her own bafflement. What was the pattern of those sounds? She thinks she heard pleasure. She also heard suffering.

Once since he died, Madeline, high on half a glass of sherry, told her she'd like to have a relationship with another man. It wasn't the mystery of how another body would go with hers, she implied, but she'd like to experience a relationship with another kind of man. Lauren heard in her voice how she floated on wistfulness — a passivity coupled with hope, in which she would give all the power and responsibility over to the man, yet wish for him to be ever so generous and attentive and kind.

Lauren is shocked to realize her own wistfulness grew like a vine out of control the last couple of years with Bess. As their sexual intensity declined and the silence between them increased, desire had grown like a night-blooming flower inside her, split from reality. There were times when she waited for the deep sounds of Bess's sleeping breath, then imagined herself out flat, legs spread, the tongue of a new woman riding up slippery on the moist swelling of her vulva and teasing into her clitoris. She did not have a picture of this woman, only the idea that they had no habits to fall into together, and the woman wanted to give her what she wanted, and she wanted to take it. The woman didn't mind if they took turns, giving and receiving attention. She tried to remember if she and Bess had started out like this. She thinks the answer is yes. But they became so excited about learning to time it so they could come together. It *was* very good that way. But also, at that time, anything they could do together got valued higher than anything they could do apart. Had they then slipped over into coming together as a protection, a distraction for each of them from the intensity of her own experience? This was a part of the merger that had mixed Lauren up. Sometimes she wasn't sure if she'd had her own orgasm or was she feeling the heat of Bess's orgasm spreading through her body?

Lauren registers that Madeline is telling her a story about her spinster aunt, her father's sister, as Madeline concludes: "They say she's always been ferociously independent."

"I say good for her," Lauren responds. She has always considered this woman her best female relative for exactly that reason, though the way Madeline says ferocious is meant to conjure up a growling bulldog. It indicts her aunt for biting off a single life.

Madeline dabs at the butter left on her plate with her corn. "There's a lot of give and take to having a relationship," she says.

"I know," Lauren says.

This give and take line is as familiar as the sexual pattern she and Bess had come to follow. She wants to know *what* did her mother take? And when did she get the look of bafflement? Did she give and give, then look baffled at the recipient who never filled up? Did she finally know she would have to draw the

17

limits, which was not a comfortable thing to do? Lauren remembers she called it putting her foot down. She remembers the day she and her sister took all the high heels out of the closet and paraded around in them. The hysterical challenge of wobbling down the stairs while wearing shoes twice the size of their feet caused all those shoes to end up downstairs in the center hall. She remembers how her mother, having just tidied up the house, came into a rare temper when she saw, and heaved a shoe clear up the stairs and through a window pane at the top, and it flew out into the snow, where it sunk through and waited out the winter, turning up like a relic in the spring. That was one time she'd put her foot down.

Lauren sees her mother inside the family, putting her foot down here and there, always creating surprise when she did. And resistance. Going against her own well-constructed image as the sponge, the absorbent force of the family. She sees how her mother created a room inside herself in which she staked out survival as someone separate from the giver and roosted inside those lines she drew by putting her foot down. But could she *take* there, Lauren wonders, or was she too busy holding to the lines? Too anxious with the achievement of her privacy?

Lauren puts up the water for tea and composes herself by moving about, clearing the table, then says, "We could both stand to be better at the taking." She makes it a declaration because she suspects Madeline believes the failure of her relationship to Bess lies in her inadequacy as a giver. The very idea of lesbianism is takerish to Madeline. It is a taking of the energy she might be giving to some man, a taking from her mother's ability to boast uneqivocally of Lauren's laurels, since her accomplishments are often connected with her lesbian identity. In fact, coming out *was* a taking for Lauren. It meant taking hold of, owning the feelings she'd had about women for years; it meant release, the joy of letting this part be birthed. It meant giving, too. Giving herself congruity.

She expects her mother to make her voice small and time-tried with martyrdom and say, "Couldn't you have given just a little more." But Madeline, shockingly, springs out of her mold. She says she is looking forward to going home soon. She says she is most comfortable these days in her own "little" apartment, living with her own "little" wishes and worrying about no one else. Lauren comes alert and listens hard. Despite how her mother makes it little in order to justify talking about it, she *is* living her life and talking about it. And not only in the form of putting her foot down. It is both exhilarating and disorienting to see her outside of martyrdom this way. She feels the same secret rejoicing she felt when her mother hurled that shoe, when the glass shattered and the anger was thrust into winter.

Lauren softens. "I'm glad you're comfortable there," she says, smiling at the picture of her mother moving about her apartment in peace, attending to her needs. Basically, this is what she wants for herself.

Madeline lowers her voice, as if some ghost might hear. "I never thought I would so much enjoy my own company."

Lauren thinks: Take this mother in, you could use this mother. But she fears the moment will pass and the other mother will return, saying: Goodness, why are we being concerned with ourselves when there are plenty of others to be worrying about out there. And just when Lauren will have identified with her, she will abandon them both. She will take up Bess's side. She has always wanted to adopt Lauren's friends and lovers, as if she did not have enough children of her own, as if she had more to give than her own children were able to take.

Lauren glances around her kitchen. It will be a nice place to eat when the cartons are out of the way. She will nourish herself, not starve here. She looks hard at her mother, who nervously folds and creases her cloth napkin, as if it might as well be put away since she made minimal use of it. Lauren, shaky, goes for action again, filling the dish pan with soapy water.

"Oh, let *me* do that," Madeline says.

"No, you can dry if you want to," she says, decisive enough for pride.

Madeline is released into chatter by the sound of the water and the rattle of the dishes, as if she won't be so fully heard as she was at the table. She says it doesn't look to her like there's much chance for reconciliation, though she hopes so still,

19

because she knows a relationship is the most important thing in life. She doesn't mean to put an okay to their lifestyle, she throws in, drying a cup vigorously, but she thought they were good together as two people, that Bess was good for Lauren. Bess made up for her shyness. Bess was more outgoing. Bess was decisive. This is the part where Madeline gets to tell Lauren indirectly all the things she thinks are wrong with her, and Lauren martyrs herself to hearing them. She feels lonely as she tries to hang onto herself through this barrage. She looks out to see the maple has become a dark outline in the dusk. It's true Bess *was* good for her, for a long time even. But in the recent past, she was not. Once she'd begun abandoning herself, no one was good for her. Now, more than ever before, having consciously chosen between leaving or staying, Lauren respects her mother's choice to stay in her marriage, but she needs respect, also, for her choice to leave, though she cannot explain yet why she made it. There are fragments, which appear before her eyes like snapshots, she could try to share — the betrayals that occurred between her and Bess, how beautiful their house and land became when she thought of leaving, how exquisite Bess herself looked to her, how her own despair came charging out, turning into hope despite the pain. But she does not want to say these things. She turns off the tap, stills her hands in the dishwater, and states as conclusively as she can, "I left because I needed to." She braces for Madeline's response: Don't you think you could have done this or that. And she prepares to answer: No, mother, and if you think I need your criticism about this, you're absolutely wrong. Perhaps because she is prepared to say these things, her mother stops her chatter and does not venture into any such speech. She even dries without clatter. Lauren lets out a sigh and slowly relaxes into the silence.

Dishes done, she returns to her desk. Her eyes land on the dark outline of the maple. She begins to see how her anger is taking form in her. She begins to feel one day she will not be uprooted by it, but will be able to use its fire as fuel. She turns to the mirror and studies her face. Small and sharp-boned like her mother's, it looks less bewildered than before.

Grinning Underneath

SCHOOL wasn't even out yet but already it was so hot and muggy the new flypaper over the kitchen table had curled up. Folly sat in front of the fan in the old wicker rocker. She could feel the small, broken pieces of wood pushing into her legs below her Bermuda shorts. She stared at a page of her new mystery story that Martha had just finished and loaned her, but she couldn't read. She thought maybe after the summer she'd start on a budget and try again to get them out of the trailer and into a house. They were all tripping over each other, all the time tripping over each other. Mary Lou filling up with hotsy-totsy ways, bungling around in there. She'd leave her room a shambles. How could you read a mystery with such a fast growing up, noisy kid in the next room and that wall between you so thin if you put a tack in the one side, it'd come out the other?

Skeeter was out mowing lawns. There was a good kid for you. He wanted some money of his own and he wasn't scared of working a little. Mary Lou would drop her allowance on the first thing that came along and then hitch from town when she didn't have change for the bus. Folly felt her worries about that girl as regular as clothes getting dirty. She remembered nursing them all in the wicker rocker. Mary Lou nibbling at her nipple.

21

Seemed like the other two had taken more easily to it.

Mary Lou came out in her cut-offs that she'd sat fringing for two hours the night before. She wore a skimpy T-shirt and a scarf tied around the crown of her head as if she were going out to sweat in the fields. "Did you sleep some today, Momma?"

"Not much. Too hot." Folly worked the night shift at the factory, putting zippers in polyester pants. She looked back down at her page.

"Yuck. Do we have to have that stupid flypaper right over the table?"

"Mind your own business, sister. I don't see ya'll working out with the fly swatter, ever. That's the reason we need it."

Mary Lou stood sneering at the yellow strip and didn't answer. Folly had to admire the way her daughter's body had grown so nice and tall and lean. Graceful, too, as it perched on the uppermost portion of childhood. Her hair was brown — short and curly and soft around her face, and her eyes were green and full of clarity, seeing always the nakedness of things — the flypaper, the ratty condition of the sofa, worn so the stuffing showed through in the pattern of the backs of a pair of legs. Mary Lou saw these measures as their failures, and with some shame that they didn't have better, Folly sensed. Her face was so clear, so young and open and unmarked, except for the occasional pimple which she attended to and fussed over as if her pretty puss was the mainstay of the entire family. Folly remembered holding this baby, herself not much older than Mary Lou was now, landing kisses all up and down the child's face, tears in her eyes at the wonder of this soft baby skin having come from her, almost as if she were kissing herself.

Mary Lou did a sort of reverse curtsy, going up on her toes and putting her hands behind her back and said, "See ya later."

"Where you goin'?"

"Out."

"Out where?"

"To town."

"You stay away from the A & P, you hear, child?"

Mary Lou didn't answer.

"I don't want you hangin' around with that Lenore. She's

too old for you."

"Mom, she's only nineteen," Mary Lou said, exasperation puckering the corners of her mouth.

"That's too old. You're sixteen."

"You don't have to tell me how old I am."

"Who told you she was nineteen, anyhow?" Folly asked. "She's been around that store for at least four years now."

"I know. That's 'cause she dropped out of school the end of tenth grade."

"That's what I mean. I don't want you runnin' with that sort. She'll be givin' you ideas about droppin' out of school."

"But Ma, she's smart. She's so smart she can study on her own. That's why she dropped out of school. She had to work anyway so she figured if she worked all day, she could get her some books and study what she want to at night. She does, too. You should see all the books she's got."

"I don't care how many books she's got, she ain't smart," Folly said, her voice rising. "People don't drop outa school from being too smart . . . and I don't want you around her. I want you goin' to school and lookin' for a job for the summer." Folly turned her book face down to keep the place, heard the brittle spine crack, leaned forward so the chair was silent, and tried to penetrate Mary Lou with her eyes as if to stamp the statement into her. It was too hot to fight if you could help it.

Mary Lou held on to the back of the dinette chair and matched her stare. She was thinking of what to say. Finally she said, "School's stupid. There's no way I can explain to you how stupid school is."

Folly rolled her eyes up in her head to dismiss the point. "You're goin' to school, that's all. You get a job for summer and then you'll know how easy you got it. I oughta send you to the factory a couple nights. Let you sit in front of the damn sewing machine for eight hours." She wiped the sweat from her forehead. Jesus, she didn't want to fight. She was just scared for Mary Lou that she'd end up like her or worse. She tried to lower her voice and it came out scratchy. "Look, I'm working my ass off to try to get us out of this rotten trailer. I run off with Barney when I was sixteen 'cause I thought he was hot shit with his tight pants and his greased back hair and his always having change to buy me a coke at the drug store. They kicked me outa school 'cause I was pregnant, but I figured sweet shit on them, I already knew everything. Then I had to work 'cause Barney kept on goin' out with the boys and gettin' drunk and losin' his job, then I was pregnant again . . . Then, you know the rest.''

Folly looked at the flies stuck on the flypaper instead of at her daughter. She was sorry she had gone on so. That wasn't what she had meant to say.

"Ma. It ain't my fault you married a motherfucker," Mary Lou said.

"You watch your mouth. You watch how you talk about your father."

"Well, he was . . . " Mary Lou kept her mouth in a straight line though both mother and daughter were aware that she was probably grinning underneath. She had always had a grin to go with her defiance. Folly had pretty much slapped it off her face by the time she was twelve, and now she was sorry. She'd rather Mary Lou would just grin and then she'd know for sure it was there. Instead she picked up her shoulder bag and made a sort of waving gesture out of the way she hiked it up on her shoulder.

"Anyway, Lenore's trying to get me on at the A & P for the summer," she said at the door. Then she was gone.

Mary Lou was gone and Folly was left with a picture of Lenore standing behind her meat counter, quartering the chickens, her strokes swift and clean. She had always kind of liked the girl. She got up from her rocker and moved the flypaper to an old nail stuck in the wall by the kitchen window. She looked out at the backyard, crabgrass trying to root and spread on hard clay, some clumps making it and some scuffed away. A lot of folks wouldn't even call it a yard, but it was; it was the only one they had.

She registered how badly the windows needed washing. She should plant some flowers along the back border, she thought. It wasn't too late to get them started but she had no fertilizer.

She took the wash off the line out back and called across to Martha to come on over. The two women sat at the table on the

24

concrete slab of Folly's porch, and Folly folded the laundry into two piles. She folded neatly, trying to keep the ironing pile low. As it was she never seemed to reach the bottom of it. On the other hand, she didn't want the kids going to school looking sloppy poor.

Folly's appearance reflected this balance in herself. She was not at all fancy or emphatic in the way she presented herself, but she was careful. There was little waste in her movements. She was a small woman, Mary Lou had surpassed her in height already, but she was strong, and her hands moved quickly and decisively. Martha noticed the firmness of the muscles in her arms without realizing what she was doing.

"How's your ma?" Folly asked her.

"Oh, she's getting back to her old crabby self. She woke me up at noon to make sure I wasn't hungry . . . you know, in my sleep I'm gonna be hungry and not feeding myself. Then all afternoon it's, 'Go lie down, you didn't get near enough sleep.' I couldn't go back, though, with her bumping up and down the sitting room with the cane. She's not near as steady on her feet as she was before she was down with the pneumonia. I can't help myself from peeping out at her, waiting for her to fall down. Lotta good it's gonna be if she does, me lying there peeping."

Martha had come to live with her mother there in that trailer of Daisy's after Daisy's second stroke. Folly had a lot of respect for what she put up with, but whenever she said anything about it, Martha would say, "Look at your own load, Fol, and the way you take care of it." Once she'd even said, "I swear you were born a solid rock."

Folly thought about how Martha always seemed like the rock to her. She kept her awake at work making jokes about the boss. She'd touch her shoulder when Folly was nodding out and say, "I wish I could just give you a pillow but you know old Fartblossom'll be making his rounds soon." Coming home in the early mornings they always came back to life for the fifteen-minute drive and concocted tricks they would do on Fartblossom once they were ready to quit the factory. That was Folly's favorite time of day. Once you'd come out into the sun and sneezed the lint out of your nose, the air always seemed so sweet and fresh. She often wished they lived a little farther from the factory so the drive wouldn't be over so fast.

"Did you finish that mystery yet?" Martha asked.

"Nope . . . hardly got started on it. I been tryin' to figure that Mary Lou again."

"Yeah. What's she been up to?" Martha turned to face Folly more directly.

"I don't know if it's anything or not. You know that girl behind the meat counter at the A & P? Short, dirty-blond hair brushed back?"

"Lenore? I think she's the only woman."

"Yeah, you know her?"

"Not much. Only from going in the store."

"She's queer. Least that's what the guidance counselor down at the school says. She called me in to tell me that Mary Lou's been hanging out with her."

Martha pulled back to herself almost as if she'd been socked with Folly's bluntnness. "I didn't think Lenore went to school."

"She don't. The guidance counselor says she comes by in her car when school lets out and picks my Mary Lou up every now and then. What do you think?"

"I don't know, Folly. Did you talk to Mary Lou?"

"I told her I don't want her hangin' out with no one that much older. She's a smart ass kid, got an answer for everything. She ended up callin' Barney a motherfucker."

"What's he got to do with it?' Martha asked.

"Good question." Folly shook out a pair of jeans, then placed one leg over the other and smoothed them with her hand. She could hardly remember how Barney got into it. "He sure was a motherfucking bastard. Serve him right if his daughter turned queer. Him runnin' back, just staying long enough to knock me up with Tiny." Her face felt hot. The anger always rushed to her head when she thought of him.

"I sure have to agree with you," Martha said. "It never sounds like he done you any favors."

"I was pretty stupid," Folly said. She tried to get back to thinking about Mary Lou. She didn't want her mind wasting

26

time on that bastard. The thought struck her that at least if Mary Lou was messing around with that girl she wouldn't be gettin' herself knocked up. She didn't say that to Martha, though. It was a weird way for a mother to think.

Martha sat, quiet and patient, waiting for Folly to get back on the track. She ran her fingers through her hair. It was then that Folly realized Martha's hair was cut just about the same as Lenore's. It was the same color, too, except for the temple parts where she had most of her grey. Folly looked away and tried to pretend she was immersed in her laundry. Ever so strange, the feeling that had crept up on her. How could it be that you live next door to this woman, you know exactly how she looks, you know she came up to North Carolina from Florida seven years ago when her ma first took sick. She works all night in the same room with you, she sleeps mornings in the next trailer, she knows every bit of trouble you ever had with the kids. They mind her like they never minded you. She loves them. She's like family. Folly was realizing that Martha never had talked about sex. Never. She'd never talked about any man. She'd never talked about her not having children. She'd talked about her girlfriend in Florida when she'd first come up, about working citrus groves with her; then Folly had become her best friend.

This all slipped furtively through her mind in a few seconds and she could only glance sideways at Martha. She was husky. She flicked her cigarette ashes with a manly gesture. "For Christ's sake," Folly said to herself, "so do I." Then it hit her that she never talked about sex to Martha either. Except to bitch about Barney. But that was because she didn't have any. She didn't want no man within a clothesline length of her. No thanks. She did just fine living without.

Folly stooped forward and fished around in the laundry basket for more clothes, but she was down to the sheets. She sat back again and scrutinized the ironing pile just to make sure she hadn't put anything in it that could go right on over to the other pile and be done with, but she didn't find any mistakes. Then she searched out two corners of a sheet, and Martha came around and took the other corners just as she would always do if she were around when the wash was taken in. They stretched it

27

between them.

"Listen here. I just don't want no trouble for Mary Lou," Folly said. "You know, she seems cut out for gettin' herself into things."

"Yes, but she's pretty smart about getting herself out of trouble too. Least she don't come crying to you most times. I bet she didn't go to that guidance counselor on account of wanting guidance."

"Uhn't uh. Matter of fact if you ask me I think that counselor is a snoopy bitch. She'd probably like to have something on Mary Lou. Said Mary Lou is a rebellious girl, that's what she told me."

"What of it?" Martha said. "Ain't nothing wrong with that. I bet that counselor don't like any kid that don't run around with a runny nose and a whiny voice asking for guidance." Martha shook her end of the sheet vigorously as she spoke. "That's a fine girl you got there. Reminds me of someone I know real well."

"What do you mean?"

"You know what I mean. I mean you. Remember when you ran around getting us all ready for presenting that petition to big Sam when they wanted to raise production to ninety? They tried to give you some guidance. Remember that? You saying, 'Piss on them, they'll never get me outa here till I'm ready to go'."

Folly tried to keep her mouth down to a flat line but the grin was there anyway. You could see it if you knew her as well as Martha did.

The Question She Put to Herself

*T*HE question she put to herself every morning those days was — Are you or are you not a dyke? She'd gotten to the point where the question didn't titillate her any more, it badgered her. There wasn't any place she could go, any thing she could do without it coming up, demanding immediate resolution and yet just hanging there. She felt as if her whole life was suspended on a question mark. Lena, the shrink, told her this was not so, it was just one aspect of self-definition, and even though Ginger found Lena a relief to talk to, she knew she was wrong. She knew Lena was denying the truth of her every waking moment and she minded but not much, partly because Lena was such a relief to talk to and partly because she knew by then that most shrinks work that way, whether they know it or not. They supply you with a denial of your existence but a more straightforward one than you'll find most places. Thus you can see more clearly what you have to fight against. Lena was good that way.

Most Saturdays and Sundays Ginger didn't lift her head from the pillow before noon. She knew it meant climbing out of bed and up onto the tightrope again and another day of gradual inching along. She was at that mid-point of maximum sag so that either way she went had to be uphill. Sometimes when she left herself suspended on the mattress those mornings, she had the dream fragments to fondle. In the dream she lay full length beside the other woman who didn't know any more about this business than she. They both had warm skin, smooth, no perspiration. They gave each other long, light caresses, touched hair, cupped faces, sighed, knew prescisely the location and sensation of the other's clitoris, didn't know — should we, will we touch there, softly moaned. It would have made a good commercial if this was the sort of thing Madison Avenue had wanted to sell. With any perspective at all, Ginger would've attributed the imagery to Violette Leduc, but then, she had none. She could only fondle the fragments and try to hold off her coming for a while because that would mean bladder urgency and time to rise and face real life — smack — in the mirror. Are You Or Are You Not A Dyke?

It certainly wasn't the newness of the question that made it so difficult; it was the proximity. All her life it had been there but usually across the road, over there on the other side of a barbed wire fence where you didn't go because if you did the bull would charge you. Santa Claus wouldn't come, mine fields were planted to blow you up, the boogie man was up a tree and the shadow lurked and knew. It was by learning the primer lessons of feminism that she had come to understand that her life was already heavily engaged with all those spooks. She had been charged and rammed by plenty of bulls and who gave a damn if Santa Claus never came again — that was his problem.

She had a kind of roll call list that flipped up before her mind's eye every time she tried to solve this problem by going back to her beginnings. LESBIANS I HAVE KNOWN.

First there were Bernie and Marilyn, who as far as she knew had always been lesbians and had always been part of her town. Bernie and Marilyn, that's how the town folks referred to them, just like they called her parents Dan and Mildred, never Mildred and Dan. Bernie wore the pants. Actually Marilyn wore pants too, men's pants with pleats and knee creases and owned the town store and was very strict about not letting kids charge candy on the family tab. It was Bernie who had short, straight hair and combed it back behind her ears. Ginger figured that was the factor that made them put her name first. She was sure it wasn't the inclination to alphabetize.

She had done a good deal of historical research — not the library kind but in her mind, some of it with Lena, the shrink. For instance when Lena had asked her about these women, she had said, "Oh, they were just wonderful."

"Did you know them well?" Lena asked.

Ginger had a picture in her mind of Bernie pushing the lawn mower, graceful and intense. She could remember Marilyn holding the door open for her when she had groceries to carry home, then staying in the doorway until she was sure you had a good hold on the bag.

"They lived in my town," she said to Lena. She decided not to bother to explain what that meant to a city shrink. It seemed ludicrous in that office where if you spoke too softly you couldn't be heard above the traffic noise outside.

When she was twelve Ginger's family had moved to Florida, built a house, moved in, and guess who was there, across the street. Elly, the writer, who Ginger's dad said collected rejection slips and Harriet, the nurse, who didn't work except in emergencies. That is, if there was a hurricane in Louisiana or a flood in Mississippi, she went on special duty for the Red Cross. Elly was an insult to the concept of neighboring; she rarely came out of the house. Ginger's dad attributed her failure as a writer to this. Ginger's mom was hurt by the fact that she could never get her to come in for coffee so she could get a better look at her. Harriet did come in for coffee and talked about where she had been in the Army or sometimes a recent disaster. Ginger's dad had once said to her, "Harriet, why don't you get yourself a man?" Of course, he thought he was complimenting her. He thought he was telling her she could be likable to a man.

"Dan," she had said, "there's not a thing in this world that I want or need from a man." Harriet with the steady eyes, unequivocal. Years later he was still impressed. "She looked me straight in the eye . . . ." he would say.

This was probably the only instance Ginger knew of when her dad's big mouth had been left hanging flaccid with no words, no grunts, no hisses, nothing coming out of it. "Harriet

31

was fantastic," Ginger told Lena.

"I can understand why you'd feel that way," Lena said.

It was one thing to be a dyke-watcher child when the watched ones were old enough to know what they were doing. It was another thing to be in college with the two Lindas three rooms down the hall of the dorm, Joey and Daniella up at the other end, Sparks upstairs and a friend sitting on your bed asking you to scratch her back. Ginger traveled with her best friend and in the motel room just before they went to sleep their feet touched. She read in her psychology book, ten to fifteen percent. That meant one in every corner. Scary. She often listened to the bedsprings squeaking in the Lindas' room. She had to pass it to get to the bathroom.

Ginger could see from her historical research that it was at this point in time that she had commanded her feet to leap into the trench of heterosexuality, though she had remained a virgin for several years to come. She hooked herself up to a gay man and dragged the relationship out for as long as possible. He, having just barely escaped a Trappist monastery via a blessed nervous breakdown, was still wandering around in a fog of purity. She, relieved to find orgasm possible fully clothed, the main stimulus being his leg, dreamed of living happily ever after though they both flinched in biology class at such words as *homo sapiens*. Eventually they got around to taking off their clothes and then of course the penis became more conspicuously an extra member that got in the way and they knew what they were supposed to do with it (and his shrink said it would mean progress) so finally they did, quietly and without much hoopla and for short periods of time, keeping in mind pregnancy and the possibility of defective rubbers. Neither of them ever managed to tell the other that even though that was the part that had to be done in the most private, that was the part they were doing for the public. In the end he was the one who had recognized the contours of a closet while she had denied it and thrown herself into the ring with the bulls and collected a series of miserable experiences.

Her LESBIANS I HAVE KNOWN list showed the gap which extended until consciousness-raising and the word spoken, purred, sometimes shouted — lesbian, lover . . . especially lover made her dizzy. It was a word from books, not from her experience. She lived with a man she could hardly stand. Her defenses were flabby from disuse and she fell in love with every other woman in the group. She condoned bisexuality, the bridge, but no one tried to seduce her. Lena, the shrink, would have loved her at that time. She would've said, "Why is it necessary to choose a camp? Why does it have to be such an issue?"

Lena would have said, "It doesn't. Don't make it be. Just do what you want and keep yourself open."

The reason Ginger knew that's what Lena would've said was because she was saying it now, four years after Ginger's consciousness-raising group had disbanded, mission supposedly accomplished. But Lena was really okay for Ginger. She was just dealing from an abstract seat. Her words were less important than her eyes which had held fearlessly to Ginger that first day when Ginger had announced, just after her name and occupation, her sexual identity crisis.

Ginger told Lena about the softball game. She'd found it advertised in *Majority Report*. After she'd finally dragged herself out of bed that Sunday morning and stared at herself in the mirror for a while, the question punctuating her expression, she'd trudged to the local newspaper store and tried quietly to sneak a *Majority Report* out of the big clip they were hanging in but the whole batch had slipped out and there they were swimming all over the floor. Ginger, red-faced, had felt the store lady's eyes on her back while she stooped, gathering them up, the word *lesbian* glaring from the front page headline.

Such incidents must either build courage or contribute to the demise of the external world view (if you're out to your newspaper lady, that's one less to worry about) because Ginger went to the softball game and she never would have done that the Sunday before.

"They were all a bunch of dykes," she told Lena.

"How could you tell?"

"Most of them were real tough and when they were waiting to bat they sat around on each other's laps kissing and hugging."

33

"I see," Lena said, convinced.

"And I was freaked out and trying to fake having a good time the whole afternoon," Ginger said. "I thought I was going to have a cardiac arrest every time I had to run the bases. I was so hyped up with adrenalin I hit a home run."

Lena looked impressed and Ginger couldn't tell whether it was her proximity to so many dykes or the home run that was turning her on.

"So what freaked you out the most?" Lena asked.

"They were so tough."

"Playing tough," Lena contended. It was an idea that had not occurred to Ginger.

Between the fifth and sixth innings a woman from the other team had stopped Ginger as she was going out to the field and asked her what she was doing after the game. Ginger had felt about ten years old and she said she wasn't doing anything because that was the truth and at ten she'd been an honest Catholic who thought that telling a lie would bring on some dread disease like homosexuality. So the woman had asked her to come to Chinatown for dinner with her and it wasn't until she was out in right field that she realized fully she'd just made a date with a dyke. "The rest of the game was agony," she told Lena. She'd kept her eye on the woman and after each inning thought she'd sneak away but the woman was keeping an eye on her too. Definitely, she'd decided, the woman wasn't her type.

"So what happened?" Lena said.

"Oh, nothing much. As soon as we got to the restaurant I told her about my confusion. She turned out to be pretty fuzzy about herself."

"Altogether a courageous adventure," Lena said as Ginger got up to leave at the end of her time. Walking home, Ginger wondered about the possibility that she was leading some part of Lena's life for her.

Her tightrope grew more and more taut. She found some lesbians to hang out with but she told them she thought she was straight. She told some of her straight friends from the past that she thought she was a lesbian. Then she hated everyone for being in a club — she hated labels, she concurred with Lena in her clubless ideals. She stayed in bed even later on weekends mulling over her LESBIANS I HAVE KNOWN list, adding the new ones. The list was becoming staggering. It produced butterflies in her stomach and a tingling sensation in her thighs. In between lying down with each woman on the list, she sat with someone she cared for in the past and said, "I'm a lesbian. What do you think of that?" Then she imagined answers for every possible question. Finally, her own answers woven round and round her, she felt snugly wrapped, an embryonic creature.

The next day, if you leave off measuring days by dawn and dusk, she was camping with three dykes. She was in love with her tent-mate. She'd slept three nights beside this small, soft breathing woman who whispered sweet good-nights. Her body floated light on the leaf bed beneath the sleeping bag. She touched her own cheek. She touched the cheek of the woman lying next to her. No questions came. She was a lesbian.

Corsage

LESLIE woke but stayed in bed, eyes closed, waiting for the alarm. The morning light was so bright it blasted right through her eyelids. Though she prized having the bed by the window, this day the sun was too penetrating. It made her feel edgy, as if she were being watched, though Melissa seemed still to be sleeping.

Her stomach was full of fear overturned on top of excitement, the same as it had been the day before when she'd gotten the note from the principal's office. She'd been in Algebra, sleepy both from lunch and from the drone in Mr. Jones' voice as he worked toward solving the problem on the board. Her sleepiness had contributed to how it had seemed unreal when the student assistant came in and handed her the folded piece of paper. She had never been the sort to get messages in school. Mindy Roberts had got one when her brother shot himself. She'd seen other kids get them, then follow the messenger out of the room, and she never knew what'd happened to them, though she'd kept her ears open, hoping to hear. She read the note to see if she had to leave the room. It said she was one of the top five students in her junior high graduating class and she would receive an award for this in assembly the next day. She stuck it haphazardly in the back of her notebook and zeroed back in on the algebra problem. She thought she might have misread the note. Or perhaps she'd read it right, but it had been mistakenly delivered to the wrong person.

Shelby caught her racing out when the bell rang and asked, "What's the matter?"

"Nothing," Leslie said, then, "Wait, I'll show you." She leafed through the back pages of her notebook, worrying she'd lost the note already, but found it and watched as Shelby read it.

"Hey, this is great," Shelby said. "I guess I should be proud to be your friend."

"I guess so," Leslie said, flashing a quick smile.

"I always knew you were a brain," Shelby said triumphantly.

In the dark of the toilet stall in the girl's room, Leslie let Shelby's pride billow out in her chest. Wow. She was secretly impressed. She'd always been a good student but quiet about it, no trouble to the teachers. A good half of her motivation was to never stand out as someone who didn't know the answer. The other half was how she'd discovered learning was like the window over her bed, a place to see out.

The alarm rang, and Melissa sprang into the day. Leslie pulled the sheet over her face until Melissa had gone into the bathroom, then inched herself out of bed and checked herself in the mirror. Strange how normal she looked even when she was nearly paralyzed with panic. How was she going to make it up those stairs and across the stage without tripping all over the place? One thing that calmed her: Melissa wouldn't be there. Melissa was in high school.

Leslie stared with dread into her closet, her body impatient with the discomfort she predicted feeling in most any of her clothes. What she had worn to bed was what she liked best — a football jersey, bright red with white letters across the chest and back: number 14. Though loose on her shoulders, it made them look square, even dropped slightly forward the way she liked to hold them. "Shoulders back, chest forward, don't be ashamed of your bosom," her mother was always saying. She wasn't ashamed of her bosom. She was ashamed of her mother's archaic way of describing it. She had two little blooms growing on her chest and she didn't always feel like showing them to the world. She liked to sometimes keep new changes to herself.

She studied herself in the mirror again. Her hips were slim. She stood in an angular pose, all her weight on one foot, so the jersey hung on her hip and showed her form. She put her hand on the other hip. Tough. It made her look like someone who knew what she was doing. Her face was too easy; it didn't match her body. It showed fear. It showed the little girl she hadn't been able to grow out of yet. She had a lot of freckles, which she considered childish. She thought she could like herself better with a different kind of skin. She wished she could get a good suntan so she could blush without being noticed, but if she stayed out too long, she only got a burn.

She wished she were a boy so she could wear pants to the assembly. She'd be less vulnerable. So many things could happen to you in a skirt. You could get your period and have blood run down your legs before you knew it. You could fall and have your underpants show. Engrossed in your own thinking, you could sit wrong and be called loose. You could get it wrinkled on your bicycle and not know how the back looked until someone tapped your shoulder and told you, and even then there was nothing you could do about it.

She went back to the closet and began a second shuffle through her clothes, desperation growing. Okay, she preached to herself, you *have* nothing perfect. So what can you settle for? The grey shirt with the button-down collar? No. Though she liked it, it had that hand-me-down imprint in her mind, and since for some unknown reason, Melissa, despite being every bit as smart as her, hadn't won this award last year, she wasn't going to wear any of her hand-me-downs. That cut her choices to about half of her clothes. She picked out the navy blue skirt with the narrow white belt that fit through the loops at the waist and the white shirt she'd gotten from Shelby's brother when he'd outgrown it and Shelby hadn't wanted it because it was a boy's shirt — it buttoned on the wrong side and the sleeves required cufflinks.

Melissa returned while Leslie was putting the shirt on and said, "You shouldn't wear long sleeves in this hot weather, you'll swelter."

She wanted to say, "No, I won't. I'll be up on stage in the air conditioned auditorium, gracefully receiving my award." Instead she said, "I'll roll them up, I always do."

Melissa didn't mention the award. One never knew in Leslie's family when people were having a lapse of memory, and while Melissa was reputed to have the best memory of them all, Leslie wouldn't have been surprised if she'd, almost deliberately, down right begrudgingly, forgotten this was the day for the award.

Fourth period, Leslie had been hit with a pop quiz in Civics — Mrs. Morrow's reminder that school wasn't out quite yet despite the way the midday heat bore down, making the earth smell strong of summer. As usual, she sat by the window. She bounced her foot with the jittery feeling she'd had all day waiting out the periods until sixth, when the assembly would occur. The heat was a drag but it calmed her; it slowed down the spinning of the panic wheels which turned inside her like the innards of a clock. She didn't see the student assistant coming, but suddenly there was someone beside her desk, a thin form of a girl. And when she looked up, she saw the neat paper with her name written on it. She felt as if she were having a lapse of memory herself. Hadn't this just happened to her the day before?

This time she *was* supposed to get up and follow. It took her a moment to work her legs. All the wheels inside speeded up and she didn't feel the floor beneath her feet as she followed her out. She worried should she tell Mrs. Morrow she hadn't finished her quiz, but the girl, whose name was Grace, signaled her with her finger, and the signal made her feel she was Grace's possession. She didn't know her. She knew she was an eighth grader. She knew this time it must be something awful; it must be whatever she'd thought it would be last time.

At the end of the corridor where they turned up toward the principal's office, the full strength of the sun entered her eyes before she could reach up to shade them. This was the only thing that made her unsure her mother was standing in the outer

40

office, her white uniform so, so white, her white shoes (polished that very morning before Leslie had even been awake) shining out the same white purity. Grace opened the door and held it for Leslie and heard only Leslie's gasp and, "Mom, what are you doing here?" before going on through to the principal's office. Leslie had an impulse to continue after her, passing by the woman in white.

"I brought you something," her mother chirped, too loud and cheery for Leslie's comfort.

"Nothing's wrong?" Leslie asked.

Her mother shook her head and smiled. Leslie was confused. Mothers didn't just come to school and call their kids out of class for nothing. Why didn't her mother know that?

"I'm trying to get off early enough to come to your assembly but in case I'm not able to, I brought you something to show how proud I am of you." Leslie's mother took a shiny white box out of a shopping bag and set it on the formica shelf, meant to hold kids' books and papers. She lifted out a large corsage and held it up to Leslie, caressing the petals of the carnations as she embraced them with her eyes.

"Oh, it's pretty. Aren't they pretty flowers." Leslie took it and smelled the flowers and looked it over carefully. In the aftermath of her words she recognized the imitation of how her mother would receive a gift. Even her voice had changed to sound like her mother's. She changed it back then, saying, "Thank you. That was nice of you." She handed her mother the corsage. "Could you please take it home for me?"

"Well, I thought you would wear it. I didn't get it to put in the refrigerator."

"But Mom, *nobody* wears a corsage around here, except for prom and we already had that last week." Leslie had thought she was finished with that wound. She hadn't gone because she hadn't been asked. Once the night itself was over, she'd emerged to face the world, telling herself she'd never have to think of it again. Now her mother wanted her to wear a prom corsage — probably purchased on sale at the florist's — to assembly. She felt so steamy hot, as if she were going to break into an oozing sweat any minute.

41

"You don't have to do things or not do things because everyone else does. It's your special day, your day to stand out, and I want you to wear this so when you go up for your award, everyone will know, someone thinks you're special."

"They'll already know," Leslie whispered to keep from shouting. She shifted her weight to her right hip as she had in the mirror to look tough and convincing. "They'll know enough."

Her mother brought forth her full scale guilt voice to counteract Leslie's posture. She looked hurt but crusty with her unwillingness to show it. "You don't want them to know you have a mother who cares?"

Leslie'd been accused; she wasn't required to answer. She didn't really want them to know anything about her mother. She wanted a mother who would be in the assembly, quietly watching, sending her a silent vote of assurance that she could walk across the stage without tripping. She wanted a mother dressed in street clothes so she wouldn't stand out, making it look as if a hospital had appeared in their midst. She wanted a mother who would tell her in the privacy of home how proud she was. Not here where the Civics quiz sat half done on her desk and everyone would want to know why she'd been called out, and the corsage was stuck between them, growing gigantic and less and less real with the passage of time. The flowers looked phony. Blues ones, pink ones. Leslie was sickened by the sweet odor that hung in the close air. She hardly recognized she was capable of such irreverence, but she thought it was a truly ugly corsage. She stood so that her body blocked it from the view of anyone walking by the office. She felt like a basketball guard, alert for a quick move.

But she was not quick enough. "Just let me see how it looks," her mother said, reaching forward to pin it onto the right side of Leslie's shirt, which had a pocket on the left. Leslie felt like the donkey in pin-the-tail-on-the-donkey. The corsage pulled the shirt down and hung heavy on her small, round breast.

"No," she said, removing it. She laid it gently down to rest in its box.

"You keep it and decide," her mother said. "Think about it

between now and then, and maybe you'll have a change of heart.''

"I can't, Mom. I don't have anywhere to put it. I can't carry it into class, and I don't have time to go to my locker — I'm in the middle of a quiz in Civics.'' Her face was turning red: so much heat and desperation. She didn't want it to show. "Please," she said, shoving the box toward her mother. "Take it. I'm sorry.''

But her mother slid it back toward her. "You take it. You're such a smart girl, you'll find some place for it.'' Her mother picked up her bag to leave.

Leslie was amazed how the words sprung out of her just in time. "If you leave it here, I'll throw it in the trash.'' She didn't want to hurt her more but saw that she had. She saw, as well, how the crust of her mother's expression hardened. Why couldn't her mother see she wasn't giving her any way out? Her mind was racing around, searching for a way to make this not be happening the way it was, seeking a cubbyhole somewhere in which to place this creepy corsage. She weighed her willingness to do whatever might make her mother feel better. Could she stand to make a fool of herself? Could she wear it to assembly, but take it off when she had to go up and get the prize? But that wouldn't satisfy her mother anyway. She wanted her to parade in it. Could she lie and say she'd worn it, while throwing it away? How then could she explain why she wasn't bringing it home? What good was a lie anyway? Underneath a lie you could only be fooled if you were willing to pretend things were different than they were.

No, awful as she felt, she wouldn't lie. She shifted her weight from where the heat was burning through the sole of her right foot.

Her mother's voice was wavery, wilted. "I have to go. I've spent my entire lunch hour coming up here . . . for this.'' She flicked her hand through the air to dismiss Leslie, then jabbed, "Melissa would have worn it proudly.''

Leslie felt slapped. She remembered shock splintering the air the day Shelby's mother had suddenly turned into a viper, her hand darting forward with the speed of a snake's tongue to strike Shelby's face. She had watched the handprint come up gradually on Shelby's sallow skin, while Shelby and her mother had stood, eyes locked, steaming.

She wished her mother would slap her. It would help release her to move. She would rather have a handprint than this great numbing blush which stiffened her even while it made her feel like putty. She was afraid to speak, afraid if she did her mother would have another strike. She picked up the box, which nearly flew away it was so light. She felt too light herself, as if she were disappearing. She handed it to her mother, who took it. Leslie was satisfied that it was out of her hands. Now she only needed to turn and walk away. Hold her face together. Keep that little girl out of it. Get back to Civics and finish her quiz. She was full of determination, yet she couldn't move. She couldn't peel herself apart from her mother. She noticed how her mother's shoulders were held too rigidly, as if she had a spring wound up at the center of her back, and how the waist of her uniform was belted so it showed her stomach was trim and held in.

They stood and sang "America the Beautiful" to open the assembly. Singing with the rest gave her the sense of a belonger and when she sang, "God shed his grace on thee," her throat lumped up with a sweet kind of pain. As they were being seated, she turned to scan the audience. She was sure her mother wouldn't be there; still she had a precious fantasy in which her mother would realize she had wronged Leslie and leave the hospital, regardless of her work, to show up and watch her get her award.

She ran the fantasy through and let it float off from her. Then slowly, methodically, and with the victorious satisfaction of defiance, she unrolled her shirt sleeves and fixed the cuffs neatly with the cufflinks. The shirt had brought on her mother's last stab, which had made the break that let Leslie walk away. "What's *this* you're wearing for a special occasion?" Her mother'd fingered the rolled up sleeve. "I don't even know where you got this."

"You don't need to. It's mine," Leslie had replied.

Her mother had drilled her, going for the final word as she

was about to clear the door. "Shoulders back," she'd commanded and Leslie's body had stiffened obediently.

Mr. Harrison ran through a string of announcements, but Leslie hadn't heard a word until her name. She had to sidestep an obstacle path of knees to make it to the aisle. She concentrated on how the stiff, bright cuffs looked against the dark blue of her skirt as she held her hands folded in front of her and carefully placed one foot ahead of the other. She could hardly tell it was her moving, but someone in her body was going forward. Five steps up. She went to the center of the stage where Mr. Harrison handed her a flat piece of paper with a large gold medal stamped onto it. She felt in awe of the child who received it. She took one quick look out on the vast sea of people and listened to the noise and realized they were clapping for her. Just for the second she could spare to wish it without tears, she wished her mother was there.

She held her shoulders just so, the way she held them in her football jersey, as she walked back across the stage and eased down the stairs and down the aisle. She felt as if there were a bird inside her, flying. The bird said: you thought you'd fall on your face and you were actually graceful. The bird said: I heard them clapping for you.

Back in her seat, resuming ordinary life, she stared at the paper. The girl beside her said, "Let's see," and Leslie handed it over. Then she wished she hadn't because that girl gave it to the next one, and it was moving down the row, and Leslie's hands, sitting on her lap, felt so empty. Her mother always accused her imagination of being overly active, and perhaps she was right, because the shiny white corsage box appeared there to take up the empty space.

She dreaded having to go home to the corsage, how it would be in the refrigerator, wilting away for days. The pink tissue paper sticking out the edges of the box would get soiled from the food passing by it, and periodically her mother would take the corsage itself out and pluck away the deadest petals to freshen it up. If Leslie had any luck, this ritual of worship wouldn't take place before her eyes. Who would finally throw it away? Probably

Melissa. Melissa, for her own reasons, would get sick of it taking up space and remove it from where it sat like the rotting thing it was between Leslie and her mother and dump it. Leslie imagined how she would step on it to squish it down in the trash can and the weak seams of the box would split open, revealing to anyone who wanted to see that it was nothing but an old, dead corsage.

Wilderness Journal

MARTY leaned back into the couch, closed her eyes, and concentrated on the silence, which was broken by the coo of an owl up over the hill. The coo made her ache with yearning. The night beckoned her to depart. Yet the tension in her body held her flat against her desire to move, as if someone were holding her at gunpoint, saying, "Death to you if you move." Hester, at the other end of the couch, turned slightly toward her, looking hollow, not home in her body. Her dark, frizzy hair, normally a frame for the beauty in her face, stood out alarmingly, as if it were made that way by static in the room. Her chin jutted forward and appeared excessively wide.

Marty swallowed, set her narrow jaw rigidly to keep her lips from quivering, and rose, in spite of the potent explosive possibilities. She poked down the things in her pack, zipped it, then hitched it on her back. She went to the hall and picked up her sleeping bag, her foam pad, her pillow and the Coleman stove. Hands full, she had to set the Coleman back down to open the screen door.

"Do you wish to take one of the dogs?" Hester asked from the couch, as if they were strangers, not mutual dog owners of many years.

"Nope," Marty answered, choosing the casual form to defy

Hester's tone. Her word echoed in the center hall, and the echo made her legs go weak. It took her back to the first time they'd ever come to this house, when she'd shouted in this hall and heard that resonance, which she'd taken as a welcome.

"I'm going." She aimed her declaration through the living-room door so she wouldn't have to hear the echo again.

Silence. No response. No resonance. Marty felt a huge vacancy in her mid-section. She wished it didn't have to be this way. The tension was still so much like a gun trained on her that her heart jumped when the screen door slapped shut behind her.

Across the road she entered the path she'd chopped the day before with a scythe. It was narrow and the briars stuck against her pants and shirt sleeves as if they wanted to hold her back. She tried to beam the flashlight straight on the path but her hand was unsteady. Quickly the hill rose, the light from the porch disappeared, and the night was very dark. Despite how she was loaded down with all her gear, she had the sense of being lighter as she gained distance from the house. She even had a momentary flash of adventure, but almost immediately, adventure was replaced by panic. She'd taken this route up the hill only twice before — once when she'd gone to scout out a place for herself, and then that afternoon when she'd taken the tent and set up a camp. Never had she been there at night.

She passed the last of the briars and entered the thick woods, where the ground was spongy with pine needles and decaying branches. The humidity was heavy and sweat ran on her face. She was overdressed, but her long sleeves were the only protection she had from the mosquitoes. The hill felt as if it were a wall — too steep, and frequently she lost her footing and slid downward as the earth went out from under her. What kept printing in her mind was the disbelieving stare on Hester's face when she'd told her she was going to a camp she'd made up on the hill. "You don't have to do that!" Hester had said, gulping for words, yet seeming to assume she was in charge. Yes I do, yes I do, yes I do, Marty had breathed. She didn't know why. She knew only that this was the path laid out by her heart as a lifeline, and it would not do to impose reason on it.

Panting, her heart thumping loudly in her chest, she

stopped to catch her breath. She set down the stove and shifted her load and felt the exhaustion that was building in her arms. The mosquitoes lit on her as a fixed object, so still breathing hard, she took off again to evade them. She dug her toes in with each step, driving for distance as if her life depended on gaining it. She remembered, as a kid, pushing on fiercely with her brother, Robbie, as they played escaped prisoners, never going so far as to have a destination, as she had now. She visualized her camp waiting for her: the orange tent pitched on the tall but thin grass that grew on the knoll of the hill in the small clearing, the shallow fire pit she'd dug with a rock and circumscribed with round stones, the pile of kindling she'd gathered and covered with plastic in case of rain. This trip would have been easier without the Coleman. Why had she brought it when she'd already made a fire pit? Insurance. The wish for a guarantee. She had some notion it would rain and she'd be able to beat out the weather with this stove.

She stopped again, listened to the thud, thud, thud — her heart. Her blood whooshed with pressure against her ear drums. Both her parents had heart flaws, a fact that only ever surfaced in her attention when she felt her own blood coursing. She put down the stove, wiped the sweat from her face with her sleeve. What was she doing? There were other places she might have gone — back to Sheila's or over to Felice's land, where she could have pitched her tent to be alone but known there were friendly women nearby. She might have gone to visit out of town friends. She yearned for the solace of being in someone's arms, but whose would do? All the possibilities which appeared were rejected as quickly as they came. She had to trust that deep intuition which had pushed through stubbornly to take up residence as her guide. She'd dismissed it for months, following instead the voice that said, "This is the way you *should* be," which had taken her further and further from being able to tell who she was. Now she was on the track but her strength was wispy thin. She couldn't stand the mosquitoes buzzing her ears. The steepness of the hill was so different in the dark, and she hadn't thought how to locate her tent while only seeing a few feet ahead of her. She felt devoid of faith and wanted to give up.

She wanted to lie down on the decomposing earth and die.

Amid the pain of the recent weeks, a kind of faith had sprung up through her despair. It was a sense that her life was connected as if in accord with the universe, not just in the microcosm of her and Hester's world, and ultimately, if she kept following the cues that came from some dark well inside, she would be led where she needed to go. She had already gone to her first few Al-Anon meetings, where she was astonished when others spoke of keeping the focus on themselves, to realize she had suffered neglect. She felt shy, eager to take more than a peek, but frightened. She didn't know what all she might lose — her past way of being, maybe the house in which she and Hester had built a life together, maybe Hester. Her faith was that all this death would yield birth.

She strained for an inkling of that faith, her toes curled to grip the hill and keep from sliding backwards, but she felt only scared, exhausted, and bitter at the way Hester had betrayed her. No place seemed right for her. Even the earth felt alien. She climbed again a short way until she tripped on a felled birch, which lay waist high across the path she had chosen. Her arms went forward and her things flew out of them. The sleeping bag bounced by, rolling downhill, but she made no effort to stop it. She lay deadly still, draped over the thin birch trunk, head drooped, arms hanging, and thought of going back. So easy to find the house, to get on the familiar path. How much compliance would be required to be back in Hester's arms, saying, "Let's start again. I'm angry. You're angry. We'll cancel the slate."

Her body prickled, as if to warn her against herself. *No. Don't give up this anger.* She needed to claim it, fuel herself with it. Fury. She was furious. Hester had been having an affair for months. Worse than her having of it was her lying about it, when Marty had asked to be told. It had only surfaced now, since Marty had revealed to Hester that she'd begun having an affair with Sheila.

Slowly, Marty lifted her head. She raised the beam of the flashlight to scan the woods in front of her and spotted the fence — a marker. Once more her heart pumped, but this time joy.

50

Shining the light down the hill she found the sleeping bag lodged against a tree and went back for it. She followed the fence line, knowing then she would find her tent, not far from it. She imagined the calm which would come when she was inside the tent, the frenetic buzz of the mosquitoes left behind.

With one grand and victorious gesture, she dropped everything when she arrived. Her breath came hard and her clothes were soaked. In all her thirty-eight years she had never sweated like this. In the middle of summer after an hour on the tennis court, she'd look cool compared to Hester, who'd have rivulets streaming down her face.

Marty stripped bare and threw her clothes and her pack into the tent, then went to the other side of the clearing to pee. There wasn't a breeze anywhere and she had to slap at her ass while she peed. She wondered what these mosquitoes ate all the other nights when there was no human up on the hill. In front of the tent, she fanned rapidly all around her body, then dove through the zipper and closed herself in.

Lying flat on her back on top of the sleeping bag, nothing covering her, she was amazed at how the sweat still soaked her so much she felt underwater. A sauna or summer sex were all that had ever released the water from inside her like this. She licked around her lips and tasted the salt. Her chest felt small and fragile and her heart the wrong size for it, still pounding heavy like a large brass door-knocker against the inner surface of her ribs. Closing her eyes, she tried to deepen and slow her breathing. She heard the zing of a lone mosquito traverse her body. Silence probably meant it was biting, but Marty didn't care. She trusted this one would fill up. If she let herself feel her skin she knew she'd itch everywhere, so she stayed with her heart instead, remembering how her father had died of his heart ailment. Never one for dragging out goodbyes, he had simply failed to get up one morning. After his death, she'd dreamed she was lying behind him, her body posture matching his, her heart pumping the same rhythm as his — then boom, the final beat, and his stopped. She'd felt awed, both by the idea that a heart is as reliable as it is, *and* that it could so easily abandon its owner by stopping like that. In the dream, she let go. She was separate

51

from him because her own heart kept going, her own body stayed warm while his cooled.

She'd begun to feel calmer, more confident in her survival, when her water pot rattled. Something had knocked it over; then she heard hard, animal nails scratching the aluminum. She froze, stopped breathing. Her sweat turned cold. She remembered Hester's formal offering of one of the dogs. Why hadn't she brought one? Could be a raccoon, or a skunk. As she listened to it poke around, she realized the woods had been totally silent before. No wind to rustle the trees. Then she heard a rumble in the far distance — thunder. She wanted peace. Why this night, when she wanted to be left alone, did everything come to terrorize her? She heard the animal to her right and imagined large raccoon eyes peering through the nylon air screen that ran low along the tent's side. As a child, she'd loved the woods, but someone was always warning her she ought to be afraid. Her father. Her uncles. You'd better watch out. A fox will come and get you. A wolf. A mountain lion.

She'd lost track of the animal. She beamed the flashlight out the head of the tent on the fire pit. Nothing. She passed it back and forth across the knoll, but the animal was either gone or out of range.

She lay again on her back. Her watch was in the pack. She thought it must be late, she should be sleeping, but her mind was on the prowl. She tried to get relief from it by rubbing her nipple with one hand, her clitoris with the other, but nothing flowed. She felt like a machine with rubber parts. She gave up the effort and let her hand glide gently across her abdomen and the memory she'd wanted to avoid came before her. Hester just back from her AA meeting, sitting squarely at the table, saying, "I can hardly make myself sit here because I don't want to tell you what I promised myself I would." Marty's heart had fisted up, her hairs had stood on end, rightly so because Hester was about to tell of her affair. A vast plain had opened out ahead of Marty — sanity, reality jelling with truth — even as she heard the words that hurt her so, confirming how Hester had lied. Even as she imagined the other woman thinking: what a fool that one is. She was grateful to Hester for telling, finally. It was a landing. It gave her ground to stand on, and instantly, she felt the improvement over floating, which she'd been doing for more than a year.

Her head had been full of clamor. Her suspicions jumped up and down righteously to remind her, "I told you so, I told you to listen to me." Another voice said, "You heard wrong. There's a mistake. Stall for time until you can figure out what's the matter here." The bewildered child cried, "Who can I trust? She was my family and I thought I could trust family." Her innocence wanted to be pure. Her savvy wanted to know why she had killed it. These few moments of heightened awareness seemed timeless, then shock rolled in to dull the acuteness of the pain.

She stared out the back window of the kitchen through the many small panes of the window. The broken ones she'd replaced herself when they'd first moved in. Others she treasured because they were the old, blown glass that contained bubbles as marks of human imperfection. At that moment she couldn't spot any distinctions. There was nothing beyond the glass but darkness.

There was a coldness in her heart that shot straight through the beam of her eyes out the window into the dark and she felt nothing else around her for a long while. Then gradually Hester's presence seeped through her numbness. Hester was still sitting there waiting for something from her. She felt mute and didn't want to ask the question out loud. What? What do you want? She braced herself in the chair and glanced at Hester and nodded and said, "I'm glad you told me." Glad was not the right word but she didn't have the heart to search for another.

She went to bed in the guest room. She felt like a guest in her body. There was numbness in her arms. She listened to the sound as she brushed her teeth as if they were someone else's teeth. She stared into the face in the mirror, hoping to see who she was. She'd only started sleeping with Sheila that week. She'd felt so strongly driven to do it, as if she were bound by a compulsion to go the wrong way down a one-way street. Now that she knew about Hester, it made more sense. Though what life her affair with Sheila had of its own, she didn't know.

Sitting on the back porch a couple of nights before, she'd told Hester about Sheila and watched her stiffen in the slatted wooden chair. Marty'd gone on eating dinner, while Hester'd balanced her plate on the arm of the chair and let her food go cold.

"We already agreed to stop calling ourselves monogamous a long time ago," Marty reminded her weakly. She wanted to say, "I didn't do anything wrong," but she swallowed the words, full of her guilt at being the first to break their bond. Or so she thought.

Hester moved her plate to the floor, grabbed both arms of the chair and reared up, hatred in her eyes. "You did this while I was away on business to punish me for being out of town," she hissed.

Marty could hardly manage to keep talking. She wanted to say, "Sure, go on and decide why I did what, when I don't even know myself. Go ahead and tell me what I'm made of." What she got out was, "No, I needed the distance your being away provided."

She felt the deep rift between them, treacherous like a ravine. "I'm moving into the guest room," she said. "I need the space."

"Great," Hester huffed. "Does that mean we're not lovers anymore?"

"It's not a declaration," Marty declared in a faraway voice. "We can be lovers any time we both feel like it." She almost gagged but went on chewing and swallowing her food, trying to get something down. She felt light, partly from the recent sex with Sheila, the lust, which had roused her to feel high and new and more connected to her body. But also because she had gradually come to seem empty when she was with Hester.

After they'd gone to bed, she'd heard Hester's sobs across the hall. Locked shut as her heart was, the sounds had wrenched inside her until she had found the courage to want to offer to comfort her, though not by altering the course she was on. Silently, she had moved down the hall. So concentrated had she been on quieting and gathering herself, she hadn't realized Hester's sobs had ceased. She raised her hand to knock just as the door spun inward and Hester, letting it go flap against the wall, planted herself on the threshold and screamed, "If you aren't going to sleep in here, then I think you should get out of this house. *Out.* I wish you'd just get out."

The shock, the scream, the looming presence, had all shattered Marty. How was it Hester had managed to catch the one moment when Marty had opened her heart? Marty wept with a hurting that seemed bottomless. Hester wept, too. They'd sat down on the floor in the hall for a long time. It was a place they'd never sat before. Sometimes one or the other of them had sputtered a few words in an attempt to touch what had happened to them, to their great love. Hester had finally said, "Please, would you sleep in the bed with me?" and Marty had said, "Yes, but only for tonight, and only if you know that I must move if I begin to feel suffocated."

Another roll of thunder came, louder and closer than the one before. Still no wind. How could a storm move in without wind? Whose arms did she need to be in? Her own. The louder Hester had cried out, asking for comforting, the more she had known how desperately she needed comforting for herself. She had come to mother nature for that, but she was going to get a storm instead, and she might even be forced back to the house. A tree, struck by lightning, could come down on her tent. She hoped with a vigor that came close to prayer she would not have to go down the hill that night. No. Even though it might be easier. Always it was easier to go back on herself, despite denial and what it did to her pride, than it was to step off into the wilderness, out of the old familiar structure of her life.

Hester in the doorway had brought back the picture of her father, wavering drunk and exploding or ticking toward the moment of explosion. He had always clung to doorframes, protection against the staggering possibilities of open space. And where was Marty in the picture? She was a small girl, shrinking smaller, searching for a way to disappear.

She ached all over her body. The muscles in her arms had let go of some of the tension but were sore. She let herself feel the soreness. She let herself feel what was there inside her. A moan formed deep in her throat, and she let out the sound. Not the squeak of a small child disappearing under the table but the groan of her deep pain. The thunder came closer, drowning out her sound or joining it. She took some comfort in this. She was thundering, rumbling. The sound came from deep in her gut and was the sound that had been suffocating her. The strangeness of it frightened her. Here she was alone and whatever came out of her *was* her. And she knew that was all she could trust.

She was leaving Hester. Maybe not forever but she could only return to her if she were able to grow whole. She had to leave their house. She had to have physical distance. She could go care-take Tracy's place while Tracy went to Europe. Tears ran on her face and she rocked as she moaned. A raw pain, leaving, like a ripping apart at her core. She feared the deadly black void inside herself. She'd felt it often the past year, just as she was going off to sleep — a great dread — a falling into some dark hollow in herself, which terrorized her. She'd never been able to follow the dread and make it less amorphous. She knew how to get out of it. Think of the old stuff. The old life. Something reassuring like being in their bed and having Hester's foot touch hers through the night. Before Hester, what had she done? Call a friend or recall a time when someone had helped her when she'd most needed help. Once she'd thought of her mother. She'd been a small child, crying and crying, so much she could feel how her face must be exploded with too much color against her golden hair. She heard her mother saying, "I know it seems as if whatever is hurting will never go away, you'll never feel better, but it will. I know it will." She had some doubt about whether her mother had actually said this or she had made these words up for her to say, because it was a rare, truthful statement for her mother, whose usual line was. "Things are not as they seem. Your father didn't mean what he said. I know you didn't mean to wet the bed, dear."

She held on. She gave up trying to get away from the hollow feeling and breathed into it and out of it. Her own pain and terror. Into it and out of it. Then the wind swirled the tree tops. Had it just come or was that the first time she had heard it? It spiraled down and blew a gentle breeze across her in the tent.

56

She could still hear the thunder but it was no louder, no closer; it was passing to the south. She wouldn't have to go back. The dark hollow was gone, and the humidity was breaking. She felt like calling out, "Come thunder, come wind, come take the hot, damp stewing from the air and carry it away from me. Leave me clean and dry." More tears came but these were like a bath. Her head was clearing, and the air felt sweet to her body as her sweat evaporated. The leaves of the poplars tinkled like pennies on a tree. She loved how they leafed out in spring, bringing sound to the place that had been still with winter. She felt their presence now like a blessing at a birth. She breathed. She had life. She trusted this piece of earth on which she rested. She was not alone; she was of it.

She touched herself again and this time her skin was dry. Her breasts were soft like baby skin and cool. Her belly felt vulnerable, open; her cunt felt tender, new. Her legs seemed light, as if they hadn't fully grown their length and were not meant for use. She went back to her face and cupped it between her hands. It seemed small and stranger than the rest of her. She teared with this gesture of tenderness to herself. How badly this face needed holding, caring. How long ago had she stopped looking herself in the eye in the mirror? Why? She needed to stay still until she knew these things. She wrapped herself in her arms and held herself. When she opened her eyes and looked out the head of the tent, she saw the stars. The night had come clear.

On the Way to the ERA

ONE could spot the dykes in the subway car partly by the way they carelessly allowed their legs to flop out and jostle with the train motions against the legs of the women next to them, partly because they had the same flyer with the same map. At Canal Street we all got off the train and congregated on the corner to collectively determine which way was downtown, then split off again according to who knew whom and began walking. I walked with Carla, who was still getting over her first disastrous relationship with a woman and who was the only one in the procession that I knew. When the three women in the lead turned left, we turned left behind them. Carla wanted to look at the map but I didn't slow down when she took it out of her pocket. She was nervous about going to a party exclusively for women, nervous about walking down the street with this small army. Her skin was too white for September. It looked thin. She was perplexed at the woman who had leapt from her side, flinging hysteria out her arms at the warm currents of her own responses still lingering in the bed.

I, too, had only just come out, but the richness of my experience held me above the sort of misgivings that had led her to fold her map over and over with different configurations, always ending with a postage stamp-sized square, until the print was nearly obliterated. Circumstances with my lover were not pain-free but since it had taken me thirty-one years to get around to feeling the soft skin of another woman's breast (and I'd wanted to do that all my life though I hadn't always known it so clearly) I was expanding myself to accommodate the circumstances.

Carla and I were the last on the elevator in the old, loft building only because she had paused to suggest we consider taking the stairs. "No," I had said, "there's plenty of room on the elevator." I pushed three, put my back to the wall and looked down at nine pairs of variegated solid shoes, one little toe peeping through a hole in a sneaker in the corner opposite mine.

The elevator stopped. The door expressed an exasperated groan. It took a moment to realize that was all it was going to do. We were still thinking of the door as a door though it was not. A door, by definition, opens. It had become a dead, heavy slab, a fourth wall to our box. Carla managed to usurp my place at the buttons and everyone concentrated with her as she pushed each button separately, then various combinations. The slab did not even struggle in response.

We were near the third floor. We could hear the party. I banged on the door and calmly announced our stuckness to the women on the other side.

"Don't worry," they called. "We'll get someone."

I wanted us all to stand in a circle and look at each other; I wanted to see who I was stuck with, but the code about keeping your eye on the enemy wouldn't release me. You don't turn your back on a stuck door. You stare at it with all your will.

The woman in the red velour shirt suggested this was a sick F.B.I. joke, we'd be greeted when the door opened by the grand jury waiting to indict us for conspiracy in an elevator. We all laughed to disseminate the paranoia and to hold off the moment of reality. The woman directly behind me spoke into my back, into the space between my shoulder blades. "Sounds like a good party," she said, her breath the yearning sigh of my lover just before the first time she had kissed the back of my neck. I wanted to turn around to her, saying, "Yes, wouldn't it be nice to be inside." Instead I tried to gaze through the door. I imagined I saw women standing in twos and threes, fours and fives, some talking, some dancing, some hugging. I wanted to walk into their vitality. I considered myself radical beyond the ERA, which was what the party was for. Still, I expected a good party. One woman in the elevator said she was supposed to be inside collecting money at the donations table. She worried out loud about how they were making out without her. "Jesus," said the woman-with-the-hole-in-her-sneaker, "how can you worry about a thing like that at a time like this? Besides, as far as I can see the ERA's nothing but a blanket designed to muffle us."

It was the idea of suffocation that cut off the possibility of a dialogue. The next announcement came, with the excessively demanding tone of desperation, from Carla. "We shouldn't talk. I think everyone should be quiet." Then she commenced pushing the buttons again while I thought, God, Carla, keep your mouth shut. What do you want? Insurrection? You can't tell this bunch of women what to do.

My concerns were ungrounded, that is to say, while they may have been theoretically correct, we had run out of air and thus, the need for theory. It was enough to feel your heart taking a stronghold in your chest and pumping fear out to every pore in your body. Enough to keep your thoughts to yourself in lieu of taking the chance, on sharing them, of scaring everyone else to death. The only reassurance floating in the carbon dioxide was the sense of being in good company.

We were kept speechless, too, by the illusion that a breath with words uses up more oxygen than a breath without words.

During my twelfth year I lay in a hospital bed clutching the right lower quadrant of my abdomen, trying to look brave. The nurse came upon me silently with her crepe-soled shoes and her syringe. At the time, I still believed in nurses as saviors and nuns as pimple-free holy spirits. She stuck me with one needle in the rear and another in the arm and told me those shots would put me to sleep for my appendectomy within the hour.

They didn't work. They glazed me but I was too scared for sleep. I kept telling myself, "Hurry up. You've got to go to sleep. Your hour's almost up."

They came with a stretcher and I lifted myself over onto it, crying inside — Wait, wait, give me time. I'll do what I'm supposed to, my throat too loose for words. They turned me around at least three times in the trip to the elevator and up and off and around and over onto the hard, cold surface of the operating table and where was the man I had seen by a sink somewhere with the green soap lathered thick all the way up to his elbows? I had to work my lips into, "Don't cut yet," for him.

The oxygen was gone and talk about a collective experience — all of us in our nine square feet knew it, (click, as those women at *Ms.* are so fond of printing in their letters to the editor), and talk about experiencing fully — every cell of us knew. Why didn't we hold hands? I folded my arms across my chest to hold myself together and widened the stance of my rubbery legs and stared as formidably as I knew how at the great, obnoxious non-door and swore refusal to allow my death to be expedited by fear.

I flashed on the feel of the operating table, then lectured myself. If your head is dizzy it is only because you are breathing so shallow. Your heart is too fast. Don't try to keep up with it. You only *think* your lungs are screaming with immense desire for a cigarette. You only think you'd be better equipped for disaster if you hadn't quit smoking twelve days ago for the purpose of extending longevity, if you hadn't finally allowed yourself to touch a woman a month ago. My better instincts rose with this thought, and I gave myself the memory of morning, of my lover and I coming together in our full lengths and feeling the perfection of our fit and the magic of connection. There was a little celebration taking place in my brain, tiny sparklers going off and making white stars in front of my eyes and warm spots here and there on my skin. It was entirely indistinguishable whether random brain cells were dying or coming to life.

Oh, I love you, woman-with-the-hole-in-your-sneaker. It is not necessary to know your name to admire your courage, woman-with-the-hole-in-your-sneaker, who dared take your eyes from the door and look at the ceiling, who said that the ERA was to muffle us and succeeded in muffling us with panic and who ventured a roaming eye across the surfaces of our cage and found the loose board, which, of course, everyone said later was a legal requirement for all elevators. Not I. I didn't say that. I grew up in the country. I didn't know ether from oxygen. How could I have known they would bring the mask, say count to ten, and I would only get to two?

The woman-with-the-hole-in-her-sneaker and the one in the other back corner had a silent conference with the woman between them and then made steps with their hands to lift her so she could slide the panel back. When they let her back down, she turned her nose up to the hole. "I always get a good seat," she said, converting the first blast of oxygen into laughter.

The polluted air of the Battery was divine. Yes, that peculiar mixure of vapors from Staten Island, New Jersey and lower Manhattan's poison producers. No one would've opened an ear for an air quality analysis.

From outside we heard, "Hey, what's going on in there?"

"We're stuck."

"We know that. What are you laughing about?"

The woman in the red velour shirt: "Air. We found some. We're easily satisfied."

Carla: "We still need to get out of here."

Me: "What are you doing about getting us out?"

"We're trying to reach the super."

Woman-with-the-hole-in-her-sneaker: "Where does he live? In the Bronx?"

Women-outside-facing-the-freedom-of-the-open-staircase, why didn't you answer her question? "We'll get back to you," we heard. (The doctor placing a fleck of your cervix on a slide, the interviewer at the food stamp office you've just revealed your measly budget to . . . .)

As soon as we had found out we weren't going to be nine dead dykes in the headlines of the *Daily News* the next morning, we all started to radiate heat. I don't understand the physiology of it, but I suppose when you're dying the heat huddles around your heart and your loins and those other places you use as milestones when you get wet timidly in a cold stream. Then when you know you're going to live, there's a sudden signal of release to all the capillaries that have shut down and in our case we had the equivalent of nine women hot flashing simultaneously. And it wasn't just a transitory phenomenon. The temperature rose rapidly to a point where, unless you'd been born in a kiln, you couldn't help obsessing about it.

I had turned my side to the door so I could still keep an eye on it while getting a good view of our air hole. In my peripheral vision, I could see that the face of the woman behind me had turned beet-red. I wondered what my own looked like. Someone asked the beet-red woman if she were okay.

"Hot," she said.

"Why don't you take off your jacket?"

Hands came forward to help her and she took it off. The heat radiated off her as if you'd pulled back an Austrian eiderdown. It must've been harder on her. She was literally our centerpiece. Everyone else had a wall or else a door that was as good as a wall to lean on.

I listened to the party sounds again. "Do you suppose those women out there can possibly have a real grasp of our predicament?" I asked.

"No," Carla said.

The woman on my left took off her jacket and her heat wafted over and fogged my glasses. I moved over a bit toward Carla who was still white. I could feel the sweat moving in a steady trickle from my armpits down my sides. I considered proposing a rule that no one else take anything off, that we all take responsibility for containing our own heat, but the implications of such a rule seemed far too complex to handle without at minimum a glass of water in your hand. Besides, I couldn't imagine what color the beet-red woman could possibly turn to with the addition of a guilt trip. So I kept my mouth shut.

"I don't understand why they don't get the police," said the woman who was supposed to be working inside.

"The *pigs*?" said the one with the good seat. "You want to be let out by the *pigs*?"

"I don't care who does it. I want out."

Carla nodded agreement. I was busy making up a scale on

which to weigh the lesser evils. I looked to the woman-with-the-hole-in-her-sneaker but she wasn't committing herself. Everyone was still in love with her for finding the air vent. Why should she want to get out anyway?

The one who'd made the joke about the F.B.I. said she didn't want the cops either. She had a southern accent and a crooked mouth and she looked fairly comfortably settled into the wall, behind Carla. It crossed my mind she was probably more accustomed to the heat than some of us. The beet-red woman stuck to her silence. Just looking at her ear lobes made me feel my own sting. I hoped she wasn't trying to force herself to focus on the issue of the cops.

Politics were melting in the heat, more so with each bead of perspiration that formed on any woman's forehead and then found a rivulet on which to begin its downward course. The only pattern which one could discern was that the women who had taken a position seemed cooler. Still, it was indistinguishable whether they were cooler because they had taken it or had they taken it because they were cooler?

Clearly circumstances were ripe for the emergence of a hero. I did a quick survey and with the peculiar logic of disaster, ranked myself third lowest in heat tolerance but second best survivor. I figured the woman with the good seat would make out anywhere. I also figured if someone didn't do something soon, someone else would invoke the Great Goddess, and I had a lot of resistance to the women's spirituality movement, so I said, "If anyone feels like they're going to faint, let me know."

I know an acupuncture point that gives a quick rush of blood to the head. It happens to be located on the big toe so I pictured myself on hands and knees crawling around the elevator, pinching toes and evoking a new round of energy. So much for heroic fantasies. I succeeded in evoking a moment of silence, a moment of nausea while each woman realized she was about to faint.

"Are you okay?" It was the woman calling from outside.

Carla, who had finally turned pink, called, "We're all about to faint. It's a hundred and twenty degrees in here."

"What are you doing about us?" the beet-red woman squeaked out.

"The super's on his way."

I wish I could tell you which women's tongues let forth which fragment of the barrage that followed but time began with that moment to move forward again and action overwhelmed the need for individuation. . . .

"Fuck the super."

"Call the cops."

"Call the fire department."

"Aren't there enough women in there to break this damn door down?"

"Look, if you could just loan us a fan . . . ."

"We don't want to be nasty but you're just not doing enough."

I do believe it was the woman who was supposed to be working inside who said, "How's the party?" in a completely ingenuous tone and I wished she would faint and we would elect to leave her crumpled up on the floor.

"Can't you just get a crowbar?" I said, leaning into the door to try to convey the weight of my urgency through to the other side. It moved. The door moved. I would have been willing to swear to it even though I didn't quite believe in it, not until it sighed. Then the sliver of space appeared, space enough for fingers. The fingers coming in from outside, the fingers going out from inside, all pushing. Pushing against the feeling of some monstrous, inflated mass in the space the door should slide into. Slow, slow, it's coming. You have to push into that kind of resistance hard but steady. No letting up.

There were six of us from inside all squashed up to the door, funky with sweat but did we smell sweet to each other. There must have been another ten hands from the outside. Altogether, not counting thumbs, that's eighty-eight fingers. The women who couldn't reach pushed with their will. We were beginning to be able to see out — a hallway, a crowd of women. Still we continued pushing until the door was all the way open. Our eyes were at their waist level. We had only to step up about three feet and we were out. I stood staring like a catatonic, so strange was the feeling of being able to look and see space. The women outside were extending their hands and Carla had already stepped up over the heavy ledge of ugly steel. I followed.

We stood in a circle and hugged and hoorayed as if we'd been separated a long time and now were having a reunion. Even the woman who was supposed to be working inside forgot about the party and hugged and hoorayed our cause. When we finally stepped back, I realized that all the women from the outside had gone back into the party except for one.

"What did you do?" she asked me.

"Nothing," I said. "I was just leaning into the door, trying to hear you, when it started to move."

A couple of women from our group drifted off down the hall to the party. I thought of calling them back, asking for introductions but that seemed ridiculous. We already knew each other too well. Carla and I sat on the stairs to recoup our strength because I had discovered that my legs were shaking.

We didn't speak, for a few minutes except to direct women who arrived on our landing to the party. Some of them stopped to curse the broken elevator for forcing them up the stairs.

"You know I really wanted to take the stairs," Carla said. "I just knew that elevator wasn't right for me."

"Yeah, I know. Anyway it was good of you not to remind me while we were still stuck."

"I could've killed you for not listening to me," she said.

I resented the blame. "You should've listened to yourself," I said coolly.

The woman at the table collecting the money looked up at us with soft brown eyes. The stiff collar of her shirt stood neatly covering the neck of her vest. "Weren't you in the elevator?" Carla said.

"Yes," she said wistfully, as if she were thinking back to an incident of a year ago.

"God, I thought we were going to die," Carla said.

The woman opened the lid of the cash box. Her hands were steady. She was using her duties to obliterate her memories. I wanted to say, "Don't you know you're one of us?" Instead I took out my three dollars. Carla was moving in slow motion and hadn't yet even reached in her pocket for money.

"No discounts for survivors?" I asked.

67

The woman answered by flattening my crumpled bills, then placing them neatly on top of the stack of ones. Carla said, "My unemployment is running out. I can't live on it as it is. I can't pay the three dollars." The woman shifted her sitting position. She fidgeted with the lid of the cash box but didn't close it. She looked across the table at us with the eyes of a representative and spoke with the ardor of a fund raiser. "Give as much as you can. It's for the ERA," she said. "It's important."

Carla dug a dollar and forty-five cents out of her pocket. "She's dazed," she said of the woman as we walked away. Her perception made me feel a little better, until we saw the refreshment tables were stacked with haphazard arrangements of empty bottles and discovered all the drinks were gone. It was rumored someone had gone out for beer and soda. My thirst was driving me to want to scream, "How dare you women drink all the wine when you should have been out in the hall chopping our door down?"

Someone had turned the music off and a woman climbed up on a chair, rising above the other heads and requesting quiet. "Oh, God," Carla said. "This is what they saved for us."

I didn't mind. I thought perhaps the sisterhood spirit could be roused again in me if the speaker would ring the right bells and we could all salivate together and I could get rid of the cottonmouth feeling of thirst. I wished I'd brought a chapstick. I was experiencing the kind of mixture of dryness and passivity you wake up with when you've been under the influence of ether.

She started with the enemy and rang a series of right-on bells. THE OLD BOYS ARE NEVER GOING TO VOLUNTARILY RELINQUISH POWER, WE HAVE TO TAKE IT. She was doing just fine. She had everyone in the room focused on her while the question was rising to a higher and higher pitch in our minds. HOW? I had just about forgotten it was an ERA party when she said, WE HAVE TO GO OUT AND *VOTE* AND TAKE IT AWAY. She went on, embellishing her position with paragraphs of rhetoric which didn't add up to enough. I wanted a picture that would actually show the power changing hands. Frowns of futility were fixed on the faces of the front-row listeners. THOSE

WHO HAVE ORGANIZED TO FIGHT AGAINST US ARE MORE
SOLIDLY BEHIND THEIR CAUSE THAN WE ARE. She might be
right about that, I thought. The dancers tapped their feet and
wanted to get the music back on. Carla and I wandered off in
search of a water spigot. I was torn between thirst and not
wanting to turn my back on her. She was much too invested in
her solution to understand how it failed to captivate me; still, I
had taught in a classroom in which a kid in the front row fell
asleep.

Carla and I spent the rest of the party bumping into other
elevator victims, Carla saying each time, "You were in the
elevator, weren't you?" I hugged the woman with the good seat
and found out she was trembling. You never would have known
by looking at her. After that I realized Carla's voice was
wavering a lot, and if I didn't stand just right my knees would
start to shake. It made it difficult to dance.

We paused for a look at the elevator on the way out. It
looked sick, tired and heavy and impotent, a wound in the
hallway. I couldn't help staring at it, as if I was looking at my
past, the part I had safely escaped the grip of.

"It's amazing," Carla said. "The whole time we were in
there, you know I never turned around once. I never even looked
at the women."

"Especially amazing because you've just gone around and
found every woman who was with us," I said.

We could tell the women in the subway car who were
coming from the party by the way they carelessly allowed their
legs to flop out and jostle with the train motions against the legs
of the women next to them. The woman-with-the-hole-in-her-
sneaker sat across from us. Carla and I got off at Sheridan
Square and she went farther uptown. Still she comes back to me
when I try to figure out what it takes to look up at the ceiling
when everyone else is looking straight ahead.

The Field is Full of Daisies and I'm Afraid to Pass

*T*WO ripe fruits, plump, ready, whole. This was our state when we met. Our bodies came together, fit, everywhere. We felt ourselves sail. We were on a strong sea. Our fingers danced to a new moon, and it seemed as if our feet would not come down to touch the ground. We felt too full to have a future.

The field is full of daisies, and I'm afraid to pass. I planned to go to work that day. This was part of a larger plan, my five year plan, which arrogantly assumed a long future. Reaching the flats, I waited for the woman in the car ahead of me to pass the truck. Waited and waited with the road stretching long and straight ahead through the meadow. Then decided to go. Then her car came moving into mine, into my side. I moved over and over and finally off the road and soared and thought I was gone. We had just come back from Maine. From beach walking, loving in the tent; from watching the waves wash against the crevices and butts of the rocks. Then I lay flat on my back at the side of the road, the top of my head open. "Please, call this woman, Judith." I told the man. "Please, tell her to come." I gave the phone number. "Who is she?" he asked. "She is Judith

. . . my very best friend." I closed my eyes. Willed my body only to struggle to clot the blood — not against the man. To live to come back to control.

The wheel went out from my hands. Spun and spun with my hands chasing. Spun and spun back the other way. I saw the field, the road, the field. No sound. Sight, no sound. The field. The road. Out of control. Often I'd read that in the newspaper, never quite sure what it meant. The car went out of control. Alone. No sound. The steering wheel, a broken toy. Here goes, I thought. Here goes. There must have been some noise, but I didn't hear it. I ducked my head before it hit the windshield, didn't even hear that.

"Can you get out?" a man, calling me. My deaf ears came out of the silence. His voice sounded far away, muffled. Who was I? Where was I? I was a person squatted rightside up on the roof of the back seat of a car, upside down. The field was full of daisies. The man was outside. I was birthing consciousness. I was fully innocent.

"Why don't you open the door?" I asked.

He was bent over so that his head was nearly upside down. "I can't. Can you get out?"

Don't rush me, I said to myself. Don't confuse me. My mind stuck on a cartoon of a character who had received a blow to the head and saw symbols floating in disarray. I noticed the blood dripping on my new briefcase — soft brown leather, pleasing to caress — also on the roof of my new car — blue interior, five payments made out of thirty-six. Such was the environment I was being born into. I looked above me for the source of the blood, finally felt the top of my head.

GET OUT, I told myself, panic overtaking dismay. Tried to roll the window down, which was actually up. JAWS OF LIFE they call the machine that comes to bite open the wrecked car. I'd seen that in the paper, too, always imagined the victim being mouthed between iron jaws. Didn't want that, would rather have the soundlessness. My head began to scream pain. I stuck it through the window and crawled out. The man helped me to stand up and I felt thoroughly stunned, as if I had no history. "I have no idea what happened to me," I said.

"I saw," he said. "WOW. I saw through my rear view mirror." He watched my face. "Let's lie you down." He walked me a few feet from the car and put me down in the grass. "My head," I said. "My head is coming off." That's when I told him to call Judith.

I once studied neuroanatomy by dissecting a brain. I tried to remember the stiffness of its substance, a texture like tofu, but all I could imagine was an intestinal mush seeping from the hole in my skull. My eyes were closed. The woman kneeling beside me said, "Please, please open your eyes. Please be okay. Please be okay." The hysteria in her voice worsened my headache. I opened my eyes. She sighed. "Oh God, didn't you see my blinker?"

My memory moved into focus with her words. "You never put your blinker on," I said. "Never. I watched. I waited." I closed my eyes. I heard the man tell someone else to take her away. "Watch her, she's upset," he said.

SHE'S UPSET, my body responded. She's upset because I might die.

The first time Harold came to see about restoring the chimney, he was dazed with the loss of his daughter. All the time he measured, I followed him around and listened as he spoke out of the side of his mouth. "I ain't right yet, you know. I just can't figure why her. I take it you heard about what happened." I nodded, asked where the accident had occurred. "Over to the curve just before the lake road. Nobody saw. Nobody knows what happened. Emergency squad picked her up, carried her in to the hospital, her jabbering all the way. I got the call on the CB. Wife and I rushed in. She was dead by the time we got there." He stood back in the yard and contemplated the chimney for a long time, desolate.

I could feel my face swell as if it were a marsh that water was trickling into. My lips were swelling to numbness and my eyes wanted to puff shut. It was hard to move my attention from my head and face, but when I remembered Harold's daughter, I decided to take a survey of my organs. I tried to think myself on a route around my abdomen, to feel for the sensation of bruising, rupture, hemorrhage. My heart beat harder as I thought of Harold's daughter chattering her fear as she rode to the hospital. Places on my legs burned, but I couldn't feel anything except panic where my liver should be, my pancreas, my stomach, my gall bladder, my intestines, my spleen. As soon as I thought about my blood pressure, I felt faint. I told the man, who brought a stool and elevated my legs. "I'm an emergency tech," he said. "I guess I'm lucky," I said. "Am I still bleeding?"

Why don't we teach comforting as an emergency technique? As the time stretched out, I felt I might die for the lack of it. "Have you called Judith?" I asked. "What did she say?" someone asked. "About calling the girl, Judy." "Judith," I said, with enough venom that they drew back from me. The waiting time was exhausting. I felt with each new minute I had to call up deeper reserves from within.

The emergency tech decided to wrap my head to try to stop the bleeding. He instructed another man to straddle me so he could stoop and lift my head with full support around my neck. I didn't like his position; the enormity of his shoes at my sides felt humiliating. After they finished wrapping me, I talked to them a little. The blood on my face was hardening sticky and these two men took turns fanning away the flies that came to light on me. They kept looking off down the road for the ambulance, while I listened in the other direction for Judith. Enough time had passed that she would be arriving any minute, I thought, and then I would be able to relax and stop comforting myself. I could feel others who had stopped and gotten out of their cars to come and view me, watching, but I didn't let my eyes move to them. My rescuers were restless. They reminded me of my father, waiting for my mother to soothe the one of us who had caught her finger in the car door, pacing and jingling the change in his pocket as if life had stopped and would not resume until the crying was over and we could pull out of the driveway.

The emergency tech asked how old I was.

"Thirty-five."

"You married?"

"No."

"Tsk, tsk, tsk. What's a pretty girl like you doing without a husband?"

I couldn't believe I had to have this confrontation lying beside the road, losing my blood through my head, my face feeling more and more like a sponge, my nose merging with my upper lip. I opened my eyes, made my voice steady, said, "I never wanted to be married."

"Sometimes I get too nosy," he admitted, looking down the road again.

"Yes," I agreed, closing my eyes. I regretted having already complimented him on his bandaging technique.

The Sheriff's deputy came, asked me questions and tested me for a sense of humor. Why do people think that humor gives comfort? And for whom? When I felt most like a cartoon character, I wanted least to be treated as one. They had failed to call Judith. I wanted to scream. They had waited for the Sheriff to come and decide if my request should be honored.

Finally, the ambulance. A skinny stretcher, metal tubing and hard mat. I would know if I had broken my neck, wouldn't I? My writing teacher who was quadraplegic said he'd felt his limbs melt away right after the accident. My legs burned in spots, my right thigh, my left shin.

As the road dipped, my stomach dropped an infinity, the feeling just past the top arc of the ferris wheel. I was dizzy. The man accompanying me looked scared, slightly dazed, enough that I was afraid to tell him I felt dizzy. I asked him where he worked instead. He'd just come off the night shift at the paper mill, gone to bed for the morning when the call came.

In the E.R. the nurses worked rapidly, covered me with a sheet, stripped me of my clothes. One inspected my body with cool eyes while the other began shaving my head along the scalp wound. The scrapes of the razor jaggedly cutting the hair nauseated me, and I shook with chills. "A blanket, please."

Can't you see I'm cold. They covered me with another sheet and left.

An official woman arrived, wanting to ask some questions. "Fine," I said, glad for someone to talk to. Name? Address? Insurance coverage? To think that I took comfort in these questions. I wanted her to stay. She scribbled on her clipboard and was gone. The room was large, stark, and the clock eyed me — 10:05. I had lived an hour. Where was Judith? Why should someone, anyone, ME, have to stay alone in that large, stark room, supervising her own LIFE until the doctor arrived?

10:15. I could not bear the isolation, but how to call out? All my years of working in a hospital as a physical therapist, wearing a white uniform, hearing patients call out to me, "Nurse, hey nurse," usually wanting the bedpan. Always, I'd resented the depersonalization of the term as well as the inaccuracy. But if the nurses had introduced themselves, I didn't remember. Finally, I called, "Nurse." I asked if she could call my home and she brought a phone and dialed for me. My brother, who was visiting that week, answered. I tried to explain the accident without making it sound horrible, without ruining his vacation. Judith was on her way. I closed my eyes and pictured her and tried to send her messages to drive carefully. When we first fell in love we commuted on weekends between New York City and Saratoga Springs. I remembered the urge to fly, the milestones of thruway rest stops marking the closing of the gap, the Friday nights of touching and touching, confirming our feelings were not just fantasies we had conjured up in our separation, saying, "Our lives have been building to this all these years."

She was not there and then suddenly she was — holding my hand, kissing my face, her eyes brimmed with tears, her presence filling the vast, stark room. I could see in her eyes how battered I looked. They were the first eyes that expressed a relationship to me.

Just then, almost as if they'd been waiting for her too, they whipped me off to X-ray. "Easy," I said, "No hurry," but they left my stomach in the E.R. Judith walked beside the stretcher. The pad they had covered the wound on my head with went flying. The attendant picked it up off the floor and fitted it back to my head. Again, I saw in Judith's eyes an honest response, a large wound. I moved to instruction on the cold, hard X-ray table for dozens of X-rays. My skull, my neck, my back, my legs. I thought of an article I had read which described the aging effects of ordinary diagnostic X-rays. I should be protesting this, I thought. I should permit only one view of each part. But I went on moving to instruction.

Trauma. The doctors would say my trauma took place in the car, then secondarily on the operating table as they cleaned out and closed up my scalp wound. But I saw a clear line of demarcation between trauma and comfort, and every act, every gesture, every spoken word fell into a place on one side of this line or the other. There is no neutral territory in an open wound.

Trauma: I asked the surgeon to position my neck carefully when he put me under. "Here's the anesthesiologist, tell him," he said. "Doesn't he have a name?" I asked, wanting accountability. I felt them look at each other across my body. I was surprised at my power to threaten them, given my weakened state.

Trauma: 10:05. Leaving me with only the clock to watch over me.

Trauma: They didn't call Judith when I asked them to.

Trauma: Cold sheets, no blankets in the E.R.

Trauma: The scrape of the razor.

Trauma: The man wanting to know why I'm not married. The big shoes at my side; the flipping, the upside down, the wheel spinning, the field, the road, the silence, the here goes — no time.

Comfort: It would have been a painless death.

Trauma: The pain in my head screamed with an intensity that obliterated the possibility of completing a thought. Several times it occurred to me to ask the doctor: could I have something for the pain? "I have a question for you," I said repeatedly, then couldn't remember what it was. I said stupid things when doctors and nurses asked me how I was, like, "Glad to be here."

Comfort: That euphoria — still not sure I would live, would

have memory, intelligence, clarity, but sure how much I wanted my life *to be*.

Trauma: That night after the surgery I told the nurse I wanted to look in a mirror. "I think maybe you should wait a few days," she said, her voice officious, stern. "It's still me," I said. "I think I'll recognize myself."

Comfort: I looked. I touched all over my swollen face with my cool hand. My head was fully wrapped in a white, gauze turban. I admired the colors of my black eyes, the deep purple lines. I recognized the feelings fluttering in my belly: a deep vulnerability, a need for tenderness to touch every part of me. I held my cheeks and wept. I held the split open backs of my knuckles, then I held my neck. Then I felt the hot burning in my right thigh and spoke to my femur with pride in the strength and resilience of my bones.

Chiggers

*A*LONE in the tree hut, Ginny stretched out her full length on the couch she and Zeke and Jack had worked on the week before. It was made from a couple of planks nailed to two-by-fours and covered with armfuls of pine needles and Spanish moss. She relaxed. The only concern that intruded on her comfort was the idea that there might be chiggers in the Spanish moss, but they had been sitting on the couch for almost a week now, and no one had turned up with any bites yet. She had heard of chiggers having an incubation time while they crawl around under the skin, inside the person, before they start biting to get back out. Probably that was something her mother had said, but she wasn't sure, and she couldn't remember how long they took, either. Her mother said lots of things about the woods that she didn't listen to very well because she liked playing in the woods — exploring, finding tracks, building the tree hut, listening to the noises — and most of the things her mother said were meant to make you not like the woods so well. Her mother was a lover of civilization.

She heard twigs crack in the clearing behind the tree hut, but she didn't bother getting up to use the lookout hole since she figured it would be her brother. Their house was just through the woods on the other side of the clearing. Zeke's house was in

79

the opposite direction. They had chosen their tree deliberately to be halfway between the two subdivisions they lived in.

Jack climbed the ladder, which was made of boards nailed to the tree, and stuck his head into the hut. Because of the way the tree branched into two main trunks, the entrance to the hut was almost in the middle of the floor. "Where's Zeke?" he asked.

"How would I know?"

"He said he was coming."

"He probably had to change the baby's diaper."

Jack hiked himself the rest of the way into the hut and sat with his back against the opposite wall from Ginny. "Probably," he agreed. "I sure am glad Betsy's getting potty trained."

"Me, too," Ginny said.

"I hope Mom doesn't have any more babies."

"She won't. She's too old. I heard her say so."

"Good," Jack said, leaving it at that, although he didn't understand what Ginny meant.

Ginny was in seventh grade, Jack was in fifth. "You'll get it in sixth grade," she said.

When Zeke came in, he sat up against the wall next to Jack even though Ginny got up to make more room on the couch. "I saw Shirley on the bus," Zeke said. "She's coming over as soon as she can."

"Shall we light up?" Ginny asked.

"Let's wait for Shirley," Jack said.

Shirley was Jack's girlfriend. She didn't come every day like the three of them because she had to babysit her kid sister most of the time, but when she did come, they played kissing games. Now, there was an edge of anticipation in all of them that they didn't have when they were busy with planning, designing, hammering on, and surveying their work with the hut.

"Go ahead and roll it anyway, Zeke," Ginny said.

Zeke opened the tin box and took out the cigarette papers and the tobacco. They took turns stealing from their parents and Zeke's dad rolled his own so they had to settle for this when it was his turn. Ginny watched Zeke's hands as he performed the ritual. He brought the cigarette to his mouth and licked the glue on the paper. He had a small, slippery tongue. When they kissed, the tip of it sometimes came through to Ginny's lips by mistake. Zeke's eyes were dark and shiny and looked up at Ginny, smiling. He tapped the cigarette on the tin box, packing it. His hands were soft and small, smaller than Ginny's.

When Shirley arrived, they smoked the cigarette. Ginny paid attention to the fact that Shirley was a good smoker, she didn't just blow the smoke out in mouthfuls. Ginny wasn't sure why Shirley would want to take up with her brother, who turned green and got sick half of the time when they smoked. Of course he didn't ever puke in front of Shirley, but would wait until he and Ginny were walking home and then puke in front of her. And just after Shirley had been kissing him, Ginny couldn't help but think.

Zeke ground out the cigarette butt with the heel of his sneaker. There was an awkward moment when they reshuffled so that Zeke and Ginny were together on the couch and Shirley and Jack were huddled in the corner.

"We gotta build another couch," Jack said.

"Yeah, tomorrow," Zeke said. "Tomorrow morning we're going to work on that hole in the roof; then we'll build another couch." While he said this, he took Ginny's hand and squeezed it tightly with his. Ginny looked over and saw that Jack was holding Shirley's hand even though he was talking to and looking at Zeke.

"For today we'll trade off," Jack said.

"Yeah," Zeke said.

Finally, he looked at Ginny. He seemed like a complete stranger to her, which was ridiculous since he was not only her boyfriend but also Jack's best friend and because their heads were so close she could smell his hair tonic, which had a putrid odor to it. They stared into each other's eyes, watching for some signal which would indicate it was time to advance their mouths across the gap between them. Ginny resisted the temptation to look across at Jack and Shirley to see if they had started yet. Then Zeke's lips reached Ginny's and they both closed their eyes at once and concentrated on coordinating the kiss. Zeke's lips

81

were thicker than Ginny's and tended to cover her mouth completely so that she had to worry about keeping her nose from being blocked off by his cheek in order to be able to breathe. They held this lip-pressing kiss for a very long time with occasional variations, some intentional, some not — a squeeze of the hand, a slip of the tongue, a cold, bare tooth mistakenly taking part. Ginny was careful about keeping the rest of their body parts from touching by making sure she stretched her neck instead of sitting closer, and Zeke was careful about where he put his other hand. Usually he held it on the back of Ginny's neck and sometimes, while he worked his lips into undulations that made her think of earthworms, he squeezed the back of her neck and sent chills up and down her spine.

Soon after they started kissing, Ginny always wondered about how they were going to reach an agreement in silence to all stop at once. Somehow they always did. Then they had a ritual of looking starry-eyed up through the hole in the roof to the sky and all saying, "Oh, boy. Oh, boy." This in spite of the fact that Ginny was always more excited by the prospect of the next session than by anything that had just transpired.

"Y'all come to my house in the morning," Zeke said, "so we can carry the boards over together. Wait'll you see what I got." Zeke lived in a newer subdivision than theirs where lots of new houses were still being built and so was their chief scavenger.

"See ya," Ginny said.

"See ya," Zeke responded, flashing his small hand up in a wave but keeping his eyes on Jack.

Ginny couldn't go with Jack to get the boards at Zeke's place the next morning because she had to stay with her sister while her mother went grocery shopping. She implored her mother to hurry home so that she might get into the woods in time to be part of the construction. Her mother gave her the same look that they all gave Betsy whenever she stood in the middle of the room in her training pants and let the piddle run down her legs. Ginny turned her back on her mother's lack of approval and begged once more for her to hurry while her mother went on searching for the car keys.

As soon as the groceries were in the house, she took off. The sun was strong. It was about eleven o'clock. She figured Zeke and Jack would still be working on the roof, and they were. She could hear the tap of the hammers as she started to cross the clearing. About the same time she heard them, she saw the man. He was sitting on the ground at the bottom of a tree at the far side of the clearing. Twenty feet beyond that tree was their tree. Her first thought was that he might own the land. On the West Coast of Florida in 1955, no one seemed to know who owned the spaces that hadn't yet been chopped up into lots. She and Zeke and Jack had made constant speculations about the landowner who would probably come in and tear out the whole woods right from under their tree hut and build a new subdivision. She had conjured up a picture of him as a man with big feet who wore the hat of a Texan despite the fact that he was in Florida. This man under the tree didn't fit the description, but still frightened Ginny and must have sensed it.

"Don't be afraid," he said. "I'm just admiring your tree hut. Did you make it?"

"Yes," she said. "Me and the boys."

Ginny felt self-conscious with him looking at her, but she felt it would be impolite to just walk on by him. He was strange. She had rarely seen an adult with nothing to do. She had seen old men on porches, rocking away their time, but he wasn't that old. Still, he was old to her, older than her father. He had a sad look to his face, mushy soft and sad. His hair was grey and he had on a plaid flannel shirt and tan work pants. Ginny was trying to figure out a way to ask him if he owned the land when he said, "Here, sit down here," indicating a place beside himself on the Spanish moss. Ginny sat down like he said and worried again about the chiggers. The man leaned back on his elbows, looked up at the sky and started making up things about the shapes of the clouds, the way you can do with frost on a window pane or the face of the moon. "Do you see that face?" he asked, pointing. "It's the profile. See the nose, the lips? Very strong." His voice had a nice, deep, rich sound to it, a little like her father's when he told sea stories.

She was wearing her white short shorts and her legs felt the heat of the sun. He moved a little closer while she was looking at the cloud that he said looked like a princess in a long, white flowing gown. He said there were very few princesses in the real world. "But you might be one of them." Then she felt his hand very softly on her leg, and he started moving one finger back and forth a bit. It was so gentle she almost couldn't feel it, but she knew it was there. She could see it. Her throat dried up and she couldn't think of a way to tell him to move it. Her legs felt hot, as if they were blushing. He kept on looking up at the sky and making up more things about the clouds, and she had to keep looking up to pay attention. She couldn't really listen though. She just couldn't move. She thought maybe Zeke or Jack would come down soon or call her, and then she would jump up and run. *But if one of them saw, she would die.*

He moved over even more, and she couldn't look down at his hand, but that one finger just kept moving back and forth, back and forth; she almost couldn't feel it, but it was closer to her privates, over by the inside of her leg. She didn't know why she couldn't think of anything to say. He seemed so sad. She knew she shouldn't just stay there and let him do that — the finger was moving up and down along the edge of her under-pants then, right where her short shorts ended. He was talking all the time in his low, soft voice, and he was gentle. "You're an awfully sweet girl," he said. "I think you like clouds, too. You see those things I show you in them." She could feel his eyes on her cheek as if they were burning two nickel imprints into it. "Your parents are very lucky to have such a nice girl." She thought she ought to tell him they had two girls and a boy, but she couldn't talk, her mouth was too dry. She guessed that he didn't have a daughter. She didn't dare move. He seemed very connected to her, and she was afraid he might cry.

She prayed he would stop if she just stayed still. She didn't move a muscle, and it seemed as if she wasn't even breathing. She kept thinking he had stopped because she hadn't felt anything, but he hadn't. His touch was just so light, and she was almost numb.

He snuck the finger under the elastic edge of her underpants. She tried to pretend that she had imagined it, but then he started the back and forth again.

"I have to go home for lunch now," she blurted.

"Oh, not so soon. You could wait just a little while, couldn't you?"

Of course she could. How could she lie to him? She was thinking she could say she heard her mother call, but he would've heard her too. She thought it was his second finger. It was just making a light tickle, nothing to be scared of. He wasn't doing any real harm.

"Where did you get such nice hair?" he asked. "You know you're a pretty girl."

She squirmed slightly, turning toward the clearing. It felt like an abrupt move and his eyes looked hurt, but she really had only moved an inch or two. His hand had followed her, never losing contact, as though it had become one of her own parts. He wasn't doing anything different, just the same back and forth, but she couldn't stand it. She did appreciate that he thought she was pretty so she waited another minute not to insult him. Then she jumped. On her feet in one motion. "Gotta go for lunch."

His eyes were fastened on her. "I'm a little hungry too. Maybe you can bring me something back." He wasn't insulted or excited or anything, but his eyes were still burning through her. His stare reminded her of how she might look when she wanted a wish to come true, when she would stare intently across a room or up at the sky and ask God or her mother, "Please, please, grant me this."

"Okay," she said and ran across the clearing toward the road, her heart making a tripping thump in her chest. Even when he was out of sight and she slowed down to a walk, her heart went on scaring her. She was headed for home, but she realized she couldn't go there yet without her mother wanting to know why she was back so soon. And how could she tell her? How could she explain that she hadn't been able to move? How could she convince her mother that this man had held her still with just one finger and his voice and his eyes burning her cheek? How could she make her mother understand that he had been horrible at the same time he had been kind? She couldn't remember anyone in her family ever telling her she was pretty.

She walked down to the dirt road that went into the orange grove at the end of their subdivision. She followed a narrow path between two rows of trees and let her mind go blank while her eyes rested on the symmetry of the grove. She found the spot to stand in to be the center of an X. Each way she looked, the trees lined up in diagonals for as far as she could see. She wouldn't tell her mother. She wouldn't tell Jack or Zeke.

She sat down on the ground where she had been standing and closed her eyes and then stuck her finger under the elastic of her underpants and tried the back and forth motion. She scared herself. She didn't understand why she was doing this. Her legs itched and she was sure she was getting chiggers.

Ginny only went to the tree hut after that when she could go with Jack. The fear would grow in her as they started out until they reached the point where they could scan the whole clearing and she could see that the man wasn't there. Then she would burst through to elation and offer to race with Jack, or hoot and holler, or push him off balance and knock him down with playful joy. Jack didn't seem to notice the difference in her. One day when they got home from school, he was ready to take off, but Ginny was supposed to peel the potatoes before she left. This had been carefully specified in a note from her mother.

"Wait up," she said. "I can peel these in five minutes."

"I'll see you over at the hut," Jack said.

"Why don't you wait for me?"

"Why should I?"

Ginny shrugged. "Just because."

He took off without her, and all the while she peeled the potatoes, she thought about if she ran into the man what she would say. And since she couldn't think of anything, she didn't go. She went into her room and started on her homework instead. When Jack came back she was still working. He stuck his head into her room. "How come you didn't show up?" he asked.

"I told you wait up," she said.

"Spoilsport."

"I don't care."

"Shirley came," he said.

"So."

"Well, we were waiting for you."

"So."

"After you didn't show up, Zeke and I took turns kissing Shirley."

"You think I care?" Ginny said, lowering her eyes to her homework.

Jack gave her the face that said, "You think you're so great, don't you," backed out of her doorway, and closed the door. She picked up her papers and carefully stacked her school things beside the bed. Then she turned over and pushed her face into her pillow and punched the mattress with her fists. The man had not really made her stay. He had just acted as if she ought to. If only she'd had the sense to move. Would he ever come again? Would he think she would want him to? She realized she had not even found out whether he owned the land.

She inspected the back of her legs as she had done every day since the old man. The chiggers still hadn't come out, and she was almost positive they never would. She felt differently about them now; their silence was hers. But she still felt like screaming: It was my tree hut. Mine.

Seneca Morning

*T*HREE twenty-five. An hour and a half more. It's a deal I've made with myself to lie still, body reclining till five AM. Even if not sleeping. Voice of my mother from the night before the county fair when I am nine and too excited to sleep and she insists, at least if I lie still, I will be rested. My cells will be reshaping as if I have slept. But here my back screams against the hardness of the bed, my legs ache. Try to let go and blend with the asphalt, I tell myself. But I only manage to hover around the *idea*. To actually let go would mean sobs, which would wake Debra and Julie, who finally sleep, and whose warmth on either side of me is the one comfort here. Two sleeping bags for three women, one under, one over us — we are snuggled in close. Later, I will cry. Later I will let in fully the pain of hearing NUKE EM TIL THEY GLO and LEZZIE GO HOME chanted at us by the locals who formed the counterdemonstration. And the other pain.

The Seneca Army Depot has lit this scenario up with ten thousand watts of field lights imported for the occasion. No wonder I can't sleep. No wonder I see so much. I see a woman who left her lover of eight years only a month ago, fluttering on a raw edge. The woman is me with a hole inside, a wound which has barely begun to heal. The hole is fear. I will fall in. Who am

I now that she's not marking my boundaries? The pain, the unyielding asphalt, the fence — these are all boundaries. The row of M.P.'s standing at ease as they rest with the calm of the guarded — our semicircle of thirty-five women curled in sleeping bags, odd clothes rolled up for pillows. It is their truck gate we blockade with these tender bodies.

Last time I opened my eyes and looked around the M.P.'s were surreptitiously gnawing on drumsticks, which had been passed through the fence by the state troopers, who had finished off what they wanted of their chicken, then split the remainders between our peacekeepers and the soldiers. It is hard to eat fried chicken at attention and no doubt harder to digest it, and the M.P.'s came to appear more at ease and human as they munched.

It was a great relief to see them soften. Earlier, when they'd removed the yarn we had woven on the fence, we had stood with our backs to it, until someone pointed out they were using sharp, long-bladed knives. We'd turned to face them and watched them cut with fast, nervous thrusts. They looked as nervous as I felt and made me aware of the spaces on my back between my ribs — tender, thin — how easily a knife could enter there, especially now, when my toughest fiber is constructed of anger still turned in. My anger abounds so. It does not seem to have a point, but hurts. Don't be such a cry baby, my mother would say, not seeing the path she has shown me where anger sits in the oven, keeping self-righteousness warm. But my suffering, right now, is a container for myself.

The peacekeepers start up singing, "You can't kill the spirit. It is like a mountain. Old and strong, it goes on and on." Their presence touches the edge of my wound that has begun to heal. They have gone on and on, all this day and night, creating a buffer zone between us and the state troopers and the townspeople. They appear oblivious to the hour, energized by the neighborly relations they have built with the troopers and the locals who returned after the storm. Earlier we all sang "Happy Birthday" to Officer Jim, one of *them*, after we sang to Sister Teresa, one of *us*. We remind each other often not to use this dichotomy, us and them. Officer Martin flashed us the peace button he wears on the underside of the flap of his uniform pocket, then blushed when we cheered him. The peacekeepers, many of them lesbians, seem almost sweet on the state troopers now, as they talk and chuckle lightly with them.

As a child, when God seemed ungainly if not downright cruel, I used to pray to angels because they seemed accessible, like these, my peacekeepers — spiritual in that, though I hardly know them, I feel my fate bound with theirs as they go about overseeing a world order.

Rebecca meets my eye and mouths the words, "Are you okay?" I nod yes and talk to my aching neck and back again. Let go. You *are* okay. You *will* survive the night and the way your life has split apart. The headache creeps up around my right eye. It is the physical counterpart of my fear that death will come suddenly when I am unprepared — an unnatural, nuclear death delivered by this army machine. But even as I despair, even as my proximity to this fence makes this fear palpable, I see how hope is born. As we creep through the pre-dawn hours, more humanity trickles in. The state troopers have stopped trying to disguise their yawns, and the next time I turn, I will groan audibly. I no longer care to make this sleeping look like something that can be done with ease.

Rebecca still watches me. She is beautiful, perhaps especially at three-thirty AM. I hardly know her but she is friend to Rita, the woman I picked up on a driving run to Seneca Falls and liked right away.

"Hi, I'm Ollie. I'd like to get a cup of coffee in there before I take you to the camp," I'd said.

And she'd said, "A woman after my own heart."

I'd disappeared fast into the church hall, thinking how it hadn't yet occurred to me I'd ever want to be going after another woman's heart. In the truck we each said the other looked familiar, but couldn't come up with a common acquaintance. She said she'd have to go through my address book. The next morning, having coffee in the diner (because I'd run into her while searching for hot, but finding only lukewarm, water at the camp), I noticed how the light in her brown eyes was playful. This discovery let me slide momentarily out of my wounded self to talk gutsily with her, as if my guts held humor and love and passion and were not meant to be merely receptacles for my grief.

Rebecca's eyes on me now remind me of my connection with Rita, who must be home in New York sleeping. Also, Suzanna, the lover I left, is probably home now. Many of the three thousand women who marched have returned to their comfortable beds. At the suggestion of comfortable beds, I shift and groan.

The fence rattles, and I look up to see a woman climbing, sure-footed. When she is over the top, she plants her toes tight, grits her knees into the fence and raises her torso, arching herself and lifting her arms in a V. It is Janine, who balances there, radiant to the cheers of the peacekeepers and a few not so sleepy sleepers. I know her from home. I am happy for her, but frightened. Why is she choosing now, hours after the last women were arrested? Has she been ferreting out her feelings and working toward making this move all night? She is in the arms of the M.P. who tagged her, the one who will get a bonus for "catching" her, though there was nothing to catching her. The bonus system is necessary to rouse competition amongst them, lest we disarm their mental set with non-violent tactics. Janine is handcuffed and carried underarm to a bus, her legs limp, heels bumping on the ground after her. There is victory in her eyes, but her mouth, clamped shut, shows the insult of a child, caught and being dragged off to punishment. "Someone go join her," I want to say. "She shouldn't have to be alone."

I have felt so alone this year past, despite living with my lover, despite the connections of my politics and my friends. As if I were the pit inside a fruit, I have felt buried, surrounded, unable to see the sky. Once when I hiked to a high peak in the mountains and knew the view below me was exquisite, still inside me churned only the vision of destruction — this same earth after the bomb, charred and pocked and crusted with ash. My lover was lying to me, and rather than face this, I was lying to myself.

The peacefulness I feel now comes with being here in truth. My body at this gate speaks the story of a woman who is scared, relieved, confused, betrayed and angry, and who sometimes feels hopelessly lost, but now feels found. Honest and sore and full with possibility. Except for the possibility of lying prone, which would relieve my back but increase my bladder urgency.

Settling for my left side, I curl into the configuration of Debra's back. She is twenty-four. I am forty. I know her only from my affinity group, but I like the independence of her ideas and the way her hair springs out frizzy from her head. Yesterday she was still undecided about doing civil disobedience. Her reasons: the job interview she had to get home for, fear of violence, and, after a pause, she confessed — her period. I wonder if the onlookers, who were here when two hundred fifty women went over the fence, realize that some of us have our periods, and worry that we will be arrested, detained for a long time, and handcuffed and without supplies, will begin to bleed through.

I think of the faces of the children who returned with their parents to watch us after the storm, the deep curiosity they displayed. I see the boy with sharp green eyes. Holding his father's hand, he shifted his glance from his father to me, then stayed with my eyes. I remembered myself, watching the civil rights movement on T.V. — mostly black kids not much older than I, sitting in at lunch counters and being dragged away, sometimes clubbed. My father, snorting, said, "Dumb kids, don't know enough to move when they're about to be clobbered." I said, "No, they know. They're choosing." I wanted to see the close ups. They kept showing the violence, the blood, but I wanted to see the faces, I wanted to see inside them. *How they knew who they were when others told them no.*

My dad, lurching drunk at the county fair, told us, "Come with me, the car's down here," as he pulled against the knowledge of three children, hands in a chain, all pulling the opposite direction, where we *knew* the car was parked. I tried to think it out — is it possible to believe him even though I am ninety-nine percent positive he is wrong? Who am I to stay with the ninety-nine? Maybe, for no good reason, he had someone move the car to the other end of the fairgrounds. And if I go along with him without believing, how will I be able to *be* when he finds out he's wrong? He'll say, "Get lost, scram, I'll meet you back at the car." Pretend it's a joke. I'll pick up the cue and make my disappearance.

Lies have always been deadening to me. When Suzanna was drinking too much, she wanted me to agree with her that she wasn't alcoholic, or at least to shut up about it, but the more I was silent, the less I was able to *be*. The less I was able to be, the more she was able to lie.

I remember the boy's eyes holding true on mine, his small hand enfolded by his father. He wanted to see inside me. He wanted to know how we knew who we were when others told us no.

It is now five to four, twelve hours since our arrival. Before the blockade began, we demonstrated most of the day. Our march had been tense, stopped by the townspeople who wanted to keep us from the gate. I was not close enough to the front to know what kind of exchange was going on but felt the frustration of being repeatedly stopped.

During the longest delay, I had sat on the road with Erica, my friend who recently became a lover. She was nervous and focused on whether I was prepared to do the CD, and I told her I stayed up most of the night, preparing, when what I could have used most was sleep. We laughed at the truth of this. Her reddish blond hair sparkled in the sun, and I found myself taken with it. The fact that her coloring was similar to mine I took as a sign of self-love. When she touched my face, I felt my own nervousness. My ex was being a legal observer for the march, which meant she was wandering around with pen and paper and a good reason to write down whatever she saw. Erica and I worried that she would observe us kissing and touching — those kisses and touches that had nurtured me since I had begun to move. When I was sick of being crazy and pretending I wasn't, and started to work my way out of the warp that rose each time my unconscious truth tried to get in a word, Erica held me. She kissed me and there was a kind of magic in the way my body bloomed, desire opening out of pain. I was not in love with her, but she roused me until I began to feel my body as a beacon that could guide me through confusion.

I bumped her then with my shoulder, inviting her to show me who was there beneath her anxiety, but she stayed irritable and closed and concentrated on her eating. When I had behaved this way with Suzanna, I resented it if she gave up too easily, but just then I didn't have to deal with Erica's reticence because a ripple of excitement reached us and we heard that the march was moving again.

As we passed the ranks of the peacekeepers along the sides of the road, I saw Rita. All day I had quietly been looking for her and knowing I would find her. I ran to her, and, smiling, she told me she had left a note in my truck. "Oh, great," I said. "Suzanna is taking the truck. We already exchanged the keys."

"Don't worry," she said. "It wasn't too intimate." We hugged and she said she wanted to see me again, and I murmured yes, but I wasn't even sure it was audible. I was there then, liking the smell of her hair but unprepared for any of the days of the rest of my life. Then I ran back to my group, her voice still resonating lively enough to stir me out of my grief.

At the Depot gate we had gone forward to place objects and banners on the fence, which quickly and amazingly, transformed it from a dull territorial marker into a backdrop for life. Then there were cries and cheers and everyone looked to the right. I couldn't see what was happening, but I heard that some women were going over the fence. Then a long moan began to rise. It seemed too high a note for the mourning part of our ritual, but I saw several women drop to the ground, writhe, then play dead. Another woman leaned over the stilled bodies and drew outlines of their forms, her chalk sometimes screeching against the asphalt. The sound of the moan went on and on like a drone, like a vibration I imagined might reverberate in the aftermath of a bomb.

I felt as if I was a giant step removed, suffering with my own grief, which had rarely ever erupted into a noise. I would have liked to get it outside, to give it some space in the world, but no one had ever taught me to do that without shame. I have been to Irish wakes where they get drunk and tell stories about the dead one, but it's not the same as telling one's own story.

Recalling the mourning makes me anxious to move again. The pain gnaws in my left shoulder, which feels flattened and cold where it presses the asphalt. If I were dead, my bone would go on boring through to the ground. I go on my back, bend my knees up, and sigh. Julie, awake now, asks me sweetly how I am. Her face is shaped by strong angles but has a look of great tenderness. She is Irish, too, and has probably been to wakes.

"It feels like the world's longest night," I whisper.

"I know," she says, "but I'm glad to be here."

I agree. "Me, too, but I like the *idea* more than the *ordeal*."

She chuckles. I remember how at one of those preparatory meetings we had back home, her clear blue eyes and soft voice had calmed me as she said, for her, non-violent conflict resolution meant the potential to achieve growth out of conflict. Even though she was only saying this, not practicing it, I had felt captivated. For myself conflict has been a thing to survive. Of course I go along with people when they say you grow from it, but in my guts I am always trying to grow past it so it will not be something I have to encounter any more. I fear finding myself powerless while someone else is permitted to use violence against me.

Debra and Julie and I tried to talk this out when we stayed up most of the night Saturday in defense of the house, part of a candlelight vigil on the lawn. The camp had received phone threats that the "boys" from the VFW were coming to burn us out. Locals cruised by, honking and calling us names and periodically throwing firecrackers, which seized at my heart and crackled the air with the charge of potential violence. Dawn, we would put up a sign: HONK FOR PEACE, which would succeed in quieting things down. Meanwhile, we talked of our tools: how we use connection, how we use presence, how we use light. The candlelight was soft, like the voices of the women spread about the yard, and the softness was convincing. But I am only halfway a believer in this new faith. It must be distinguished from my mother's anger in the oven keeping warm. From the queasy sitting-duck feeling when we waited at the table for the loose-hearted, angry, drunken father to come home. I spoke of my presence there in that yard, yet the confidence I needed in its power still rested largely in the theoretical. The fear stuffed in my craw kept me wound up to flinch each time a firecracker exploded. I speculated about the men: they could not possibly get organized while driving up and down in all those separate cars. If the bars closed at three, why hadn't they arrived with torches by three-thirty? Had they drunk themselves to impotence? I try to gain control by making up their motives, when the real power lies in letting go. Not centering my life in reaction to them.

Julie rubs the knotted muscles of my shoulder blade and her touch opens my memory to when we sat down in the circle to begin the blockade, our backs to the locals, who chanted: COMMIE QUEERS! GO HOME! We watched our sisters scaling the fence, four and five at a time. The chants felt as if they struck me; they stung my back, and I wanted more protection, thicker clothes, though it was so hot I could feel the sweat running a course down my sides. Then Julie suggested we turn around and face the crowd, and she and I did. I spotted a woman who looked like a neighbor I babysat for years ago, when I was thirteen — Mrs. Cunningham. She had dark hairs sprouting out of her chin and a gruff voice, which she used constantly to yell at her children. I was always astounded to realize she dropped to her normal voice for me, implying I was closer to being on her side than theirs. I met the eyes of that woman and held them, and her mouth, open in the middle of a chant, stopped, caught by the real contact between us. Only after she averted her eyes did she begin again to mouth words, but her chant had lost its vinegar. She gave me a sense of possibility. I didn't feel safe, but I felt connected, both to myself and these people, whose chants said: No, we are not like you. I saw the fear in them, and it didn't look that different from my own fears — of encountering the unnatural death of the bomb, of radiation leeching off the base and invisibly creeping into their town, of powerlessness in the face of violence and not knowing how to trust non-violence. Who among us does? I have admitted I have only half a faith myself, though at that moment it filled me.

Later, when the numbers of women scaling the fence had dwindled, a heckler who had climbed to a perch on a telephone pole, enjoined us to go for it. "Come on, girls, your turn. The fence is yours. Take it." He both angered and amused me. Here was a man who had come out to oppose our action, now he didn't want it to be over.

He did not last the thunderstorm, which moved swiftly and magnificently in across the lake at about eight-thirty. The wind came whipping up our hair and our ponchos and the things we had placed on the fence, little else to stir in the sterile base atmosphere. The M.P.'s put on belted down, noiseless raincoats. The lightning struck so bright with its electric energy, and the thunder cracked so loud, and the rain pelted us, hard as any I have ever been out in. We were still in our circle. Then we stood up and began to scream and cheer, exuberant with the expression of the storm. The tensions of the day washed down, and we raised our arms in victory. The hecklers were gone, the M.P.'s were a picture of restraint, and the truck gate was ours. Then the grey clouds went on out over the base and we turned around to see the red sky coming where they had been, the sun already down below the long, flat horizon. My clothes were soaked and I feared getting cold, but my spirits went high, and it no longer seemed like the end of a long and straining day.

What kept me going through the hours till our support group came with dry clothes and sleeping bags was a motley collection of odd and caring gestures such as make foundation for the raising of faith. First came a woman who laid out a dry tarp, then dumped on it the contents of the lost-and-found-box from camp. I managed to snare a pair of wool pants, five sizes too large, but dry. Someone brought a huge pot of soup. A woman with a grey jacket, who noticed I was shivering, said I should take it and send it back to her at the address in the pocket. Then her friend said, "Here, use my white jacket any way you can and send it back with hers." Then Erica and other friends came with a Coleman and made tea.

Comforted by Julie's massage, I have finally entered sleep, so I am startled when Janine shakes my shoulder gently but urgently. "Hey, they're on the move," she says. "I think they're coming out to arrest us."

I blink with confusion at seeing her. "Janine, didn't you go over?"

"Yes," she whispers, "but they gave me my ban and bar letter and let me right out, so I came back up here."

The M.P.'s are racing about, moving into formation in front of the gate. They are clanking their guns and making get ready noises. I scramble for my shoes. Many of the women do not move out of their sleeping bags, but I feel too vulnerable barefooted, especially since they have caught me in my one moment of sleep, damn it. Julie goes for her shoes, too, but Debra only cracks one eye to say, what's going on. I am out and up and ready for them, when, on command, they lay their guns down and break into jumping jacks. ONETWOTHREEFOUR. ONETWOTHREEFOUR. It takes a second to realize it's English they're shouting, the simplest of numbers. It is four forty-five. Between sets they emit grumpy, growling snarls, meant to terrorize or humor a bunch of tired women. I get up and do jumping jacks with them. It feels wonderful on my back after all the hours of disciplining myself to lie still.

Push-ups. Deep knee-bends. This is like the relief that came when I stopped waiting for my lover to tell me what was wrong. When I let my body open to a sensation that was not pain. When I stopped pretending I was there, though I was lost and waiting to be found. When I allowed my body to become a beacon. Wholesome. It felt wholesome to be jumping, to have the long wait over. To begin asking questions: How did I arrive here on this shore when we began on such a strong sail of love? When we once were inspiring to each other. When I have always known you cannot deny your dreams or your backbone.

The soldiers finish their calisthenics, and we give them a rousing cheer. Debra is awake now, and as good humored with her couple of hours sleep as I am with my recent burst of activity. A woman comes from camp to say they need a press

99

release for the early morning news, so Debra and I and another woman, who is groggy but a crisis reactor, sit and scribble on a paper: *We are women who have blockaded the truck gate as a protest against the deployment of Cruise and Pershing II missiles to Europe. We are establishing, at this gate, the Women's Encampment for a Future of Peace and Justice, Number Two. We have spent the night here, and many useful dialogues have begun between us and some local residents, the state troopers, and even some M.P.'s.* We pass the statement on to some other rising women to complete. There is so much unsaid, yet in our very presence there is so much said. So much possibility for knowing and for living. For growth out of protest. For the slow, careful building of new trust.

Debra and Julie and I pass the tent draped with a large banner — Women's Peace Encampment #2 — and walk a long way down the road to a field not lit by field lights to pee. A jeep follows us on the parallel road inside the base. A helicopter flies overhead, and Debra waves her sanitary napkin wildly at the pilot before she squats. I tell them I heard the new morning captain answer the phone in the gatehouse, saying, "Have we surrendered this gate or what?" Who knows what we will become. We are meeting with the others at seven. Someone has already suggested we bring in a portajane and more tents. Our heads are full of ideas. We have the support women in our affinity group, who will be coming soon with breakfast. Later, we will gather with them and tell our experience. And they will tell us theirs: how they got clothes for Julie out of the wrong tent, how they worried for our safety, and how they couldn't find the car.

We walk back toward the gate and the sun is rising. I stretch. The light is changing every minute. We will eventually be arrested, but not before this light rises. I feel a deep warmth spreading in my soul.

When I get home, I'll do more settling and unsettling with Suzanna, and with myself. I'll mail the jackets to the woman in Cape May who, along with her address, left sand in her pockets. I'll find the note Rita left. I'll remember the healing feel of the peacekeepers and the V that Janine made when she perched on the fence, the charge of the storm, the pain of the field lights, and now, this great orange sun, rising where I am found.

Care in the Holding

*L*AURA waited nervously while the woman filled out the contract for the rental car. "Two seater okay?" she asked.

"Sure," Laura replied, confused about the question which barely touched down in her float of mind. What was she renting — a motorcycle? Minutes later, she found herself checking out the two-seater — indeed a car — a sporty Ford with bucket seats up front and a long hatch in back. Placing her directions on the other seat, she headed for the Bay Bridge, for her rendezvous with Chana, whom she was picking up at cousin Richard's in Berkeley Hills. Her mind printed an image of Chana — brown eyes with a sparkle in them, soft cheeks, sweet smell — and her heart sent a streak of excitement straight down her gut and into her loins. She'd be lucky if she made the right turns, so excited to distraction was she. She'd been sitting on this excitement a whole month now, since the hike they'd taken back east, which had tripped off a great glow in her heart.

She pulled off the road and stopped in the hills when she sensed she was nearly there, and tried to gather herself. Prepare. For what? She *knew* it would be good. She *knew* they liked each other. She *knew* the day on the mountain had been like magic and they were the same two women coming together again. Breathe, she said to herself. She took ten long, deep breaths. On the tenth she realized she hadn't even checked to see if the charge was correct before signing the contract for the car rental. She dug it out and looked and got further confused because they hadn't filled in the charges. But, of course: they were waiting to see if she'd return it on time.

More deep breaths. She felt light-headed, maybe hyperventilation. What will she be like? The streak of adrenalin in her gut again. The feel of energy in her center, intense, like if *she* wasn't going to move that car, her clitoris would be willing to drive. Go on. Jump. The waiting has been long enough already.

She started up the car. The next left was the cousin's street and time speeded up. She was at the door ringing the doorbell. The door was large, opened out. Disorienting. She'd pictured Chana receiving her, inward, with the opening of a door, but now this door. What?

Chana pushed it open, came out herself with the door and gently hugged Laura, who was near to fainting. Chana radiant, wearing red, eyes friendly; her short dark hair started down over her forehead, then curled back. She invited Laura in. Laura smiled yes, speechless, don't ask me to talk. Chana took her to the back porch where cousin Richard and girlfriend were sitting. They showed off a hummingbird, and the flutter of the hummingbird's wings felt like the stir inside her chest. The house was built on the side of a hill, and the porch felt as if it was suspended in air. She glanced at Chana, caught the intensity of her beauty, and felt as if the house was going to slide down the cliff. Said to herself: keep breathing. Said to them: "Exciting to live here. You must feel on the edge all the time."

"I don't notice it at all," said cousin Richard, oblivious to the intensity of her feelings.

Chana took Laura on a tour of the house. In the bathroom, she kissed her. Laura held Chana's head, held their cheeks pressed together and, heart pounding, began to feel recognition from the last time. She felt the ways they were strangers acutely, and wanted to hold their bodies together until they knew all the connections that were there.

"Let's say goodbye and go," Chana said. Her cousin wrote

out a series of turns to the Richmond Bridge. Chana seemed composed, able to follow the directions, while glancing at Laura, flirting with the sparkle in her eyes. Laura went closer to the edge of the porch, looked out over the long view, but still couldn't look down.

They left. They got lost on the first turn but drove on somewhat aimlessly. "What's your take?" Laura asked Chana.

"I think this will get us there."

"I like the way you follow your instincts," Laura said, going on down through Berkeley, feeling both cocky and lost. They were getting to know each other the same way. Laura alternated between having faith in that instinctual plane and feeling a stranger, both to herself and to Chana. What if they were going blocks and blocks in the wrong direction? She wanted to be at the ocean, out of the car. She wanted to be where they could hold each other. Yet she was glad to have the mission of driving. Needed time to establish a sense of Chana in the real flesh, not fantasy, before they made love. For the past month, they had written sweet and tender love letters; encouraging words, sharing of fragments of their lives such as food tastes, favorite books, excitement about the work each was doing at the moment. Laura had been in residence at a West Coast artists' retreat, while Chana had been home in New York preparing to turn over her first book to her publisher.

From the moment she'd arrived in her place of retreat, Laura had noticed that the bedroom alcove was more fit for romance than for thinking up stories. The king-sized bed was made enchanting by the two walls of windows, which wrapped around it. Outside, the branches of an oak reached in close to the windows, and the patterns of the leaves, black at night, had a dreamy feeling to them. In the moonlight they lost their distinct edges and became blots placed in some mysterious order. They offered an entirely different impression, green, in the mornings. She had loved sleeping there, dropping into the dream reality of night, then waking into a gentle California green. She woke with a kind of relaxed openness she hadn't experienced for a long time. And it was in that openness she yearned to wake and look upon Chana's sleeping face next to her. She wanted that openness, that wonder she had seen in Chana's eyes as they pulled back from kissing up on the mountain and looked each other full in the face.

They had found and crossed the Richmond Bridge and were headed for the coast when they came into a misty fog. This was Laura's first time seeing it like this. The other times she'd driven up Route One she'd seen that magnificent long view of the rugged shoreline from the headlands. Now the fog closed around them, and even when she knew they were near the ocean, she couldn't make it out. She'd only imagined bringing Chana here to the long view. Taking her by the hand and leading her down to a quiet spot on the hill and watching her take it in. The view awesome as the strong feeling that traveled breast to breast as they held each other. Now what? Chana took her hand and kissed it softly, then held it to her own heart. Laura smiled, warm inside. Scared, too. Who was Chana? Who was she? Why were they feeling so much while knowing so little about each other? She darted looks at Chana but the curving road required her attention. Next time she saw a place to pull off, she did. Said let's go down the hill a little and see if we can hear the ocean.

They both got out. Laura stretched, releasing some of the tension. It took a second for her to realize she was standing still, it was the car that was moving. Rolling backwards. She ran for the door and hit the brake. Embarrassed at her driving ineptitude, she turned red. "You're distracted," Chana said, coming around. Laura put the car in Park and pulled hard on the emergency brake, then laughed. "The navigator will have to see that the car is not left in neutral." Chana pulled her out and hugged her and kissed her. "Lucky we weren't on a big hill," she said.

They moved down to a point where they could see the waves crashing in on the rocks below. First they sat huddled close, as they had on the mountain, and kissed, smelled each other's hair, felt the deep magnitude pulling between them. Then they lay down. The fog created a room for them. They couldn't see the road or the sky. Sometimes they could see the ocean, sometimes not, but always they could hear its rhythm. They held each other and rocked together. "How I've longed for this," Laura whispered. "I know. I know," Chana replied. Their lust flushed their faces as they lay side by side, the full length of their bodies pressed close. The fog provided privacy. The room it made for them was impersonal, without decoration. It had no square corners, no flat walls. It moved in close. A gentle kiss grew into deep passion. When they looked again, the fog had thinned and the room expanded.

Laura felt one with her body and with the cliff they lay on. Her hand moved slowly up and down, charting the soft contours of Chana's body, remembering the curve of her back from the last time. She followed the line of Chana's firm thigh and pictured the gracefulness with which she must run.

Chana pressed her pelvis closer and Laura's lust peaked in response, sending charges like lightning, sharp through her body and back to Chana. She was breathless, delirious, joyous. Chana murmured how she loved her smell, rolled on her back, and Laura rolled with her so she was on top. Laura pressed into her, tasted and smelled Chana's neck, and inhaled deeply of the moist ocean air. She felt the hummingbird stir in her chest while her cunt both beamed a radiant heat and received the hot waves of Chana's sexual energy. Suddenly she wanted her naked. She wanted to be inside her, feeling the moisture she knew was there, wanted to have her own self known that way, free of the covering and constriction of clothes, but she knew this, just as it was, a kind of bliss, deserved its full due. Like a rose opening to full bloom, beautiful in all its stages, it had a timing of its own. She arched her head back and saw in Chana's face a desire that matched hers. How expressive that face was, how its movement reminded her of the waves below. Desire charging, cresting, then ebbing back as her closed lips fell into a quiet smile, broadening her face. Time was no more distinct than the boundaries of the room — seemed long if Laura thought of how much she was alive for each one of these minutes, short in the sense that there was no more waiting, waiting was over.

They stopped in a small beach town for coffee before going on to Laura's studio. Chana did most of the talking. Laura had trouble taking in the words or being verbal herself, though she wanted to make herself known this way. She had the precipice feeling again, like she'd had on Richard's porch, just from sitting across the table from Chana. She found her beauty so striking she was surprised the other people in the coffee shop were acting as if it were an ordinary day and not noticing this clear-eyed, extraordinary woman sitting across from her, sipping coffee and radiating joy. She went to the restroom and confirmed in the mirror that, sure enough, it *was* possible to see the radiance that *she* was exuding, as well. Her eyes looked greener, her hair looked a shiny, light brown. Her skin looked soft and clear, ruddy and inviting. The warmth in her pulsed so she felt brought close to her own essence.

When they arrived at the studio, she felt this closeness still, but also the strangeness of the place, hers but not hers, a gift for the month, and the strangeness of their knowing nothing of each other's homes. She led Chana around, pointing out the skylight dome at the peak of the building, the deck, the small kitchen, the charming bath. Still holding her hand, she led her down the two steps into the bedroom alcove. She fell onto the bed and leaned back, gazing out on her familiar and favorite view. "Come." She reached toward Chana, who stood smiling, then came down next to her. "It is paradise," she said, her voice almost husky. "You weren't making that up."

"Especially now with you here, it is," Laura said.

Then they held each other and Laura's breath went away. She gasped for it somewhere under the lust. She felt the firmness of her own body as well as Chana's as they held tight. It was dusk and the light played on Chana's face which was wonderfully variable. Sometimes soft with pleasure, sometimes scared, or suffused with passion — all looks welcomed by Laura as they broached the complexity of her own feelings. If she and Chana truly were strangers, why did their bodies seem already so well acquainted? And more than acquainted, as if they'd been waiting and yearning a long time for this meeting.

They kissed deeply. Laura rolled on top. Chana put her hand at the base of Laura's spine and rocked her back and forth in a gentle rhythm, and Laura felt the sweet warmth growing in her cunt. She ran her fingers through Chana's hair, held her lovely head, and loved the rhythm they both followed then. Chana pulled their shirts up enough so their bare bellies touched and the warmth spread more fully to there. Laura felt their belly skins kissing — soft coverings overlying those guts pitched high with risk. She rose to take her top off and pulled Chana's off as well. Then they lay breast to breast and felt that warmth course through their chests. Laura cupped one of Chana's breasts in her hand and nuzzled down and tongued the nipple and watched it come erect. When she leaned back to look at Chana's face, Chana admired her breasts, saying they were perfect. Laura murmured her response. They rolled so that Chana was on top. Chana built on the same gentle but spunky rhythm. They built but did not come. What Laura needed for orgasm was no greater intensity than what they had already created; it was the building of trust. To feel the care behind Chana's caresses. And to trust that care.

Laura was raw in places, thin skinned in her healing from the break up with her lover of many years. It had been four months since she'd left their home, their bed, many more since they'd been really alive, sexually, with each other. She remembered times when they'd put great effort into making love and she'd stayed for a long time on the brink, almost coming off that edge but not quite, not quite able to. She remembered after her father died, when she came back home from the funeral, how she felt so alone. Bess didn't seem to really be there. She was, but she wasn't. Laura didn't seem able to ask her for what she needed. More holding. More care. More care in the holding. Bess was still depressed herself from having lost her job, and Bess came from a family where death passed in silence, feelings held in. So Laura had gotten on this brink and stayed there, knowing if she came it would be with a burst of tears, that her pleasure was enfolded by her grief. Sharing the pleasure when she was not able to get the care seemed a betrayal of her body. And her body, often truer to her than her mind, balked. "It's okay," she'd told Bess. "We don't have to be so goal oriented." But Bess became reluctant to initiate sex with her, and this at a time when she wanted Bess to do the reaching.

Chana on top of her was close to her own size. Bess had

been a good deal heavier, and this position had verged on feeling stifling to her with Bess. She felt a wave of freedom at having made this choice, and the wave brought her back to the glow in her belly, in her loins. At the same time, she felt tears very close to her pleasure. Chana was rocking her again. Comforting. The rhythm was right for her. How did Chana know to make it that way? Laura looked again to take in her face. Sweet, soft, mystery. She also has memory, she thought. Of what? Of whom? Where did this bonding, this movement towards intimacy, take her? Her concentration was strong, she was all there, deeply inside her body. She called Laura's name. She said, you, you, and Laura was wakened further by the call.

They stopped to kick off their pants and then coming together again was like another new meeting. Like when the door opened out and Chana came with it. Like when they first lay on the cliff and held their bodies full length. Their bellies and breasts, their lips and cheeks came back together, familiar, still new but knowledgeable, warmed to each other. Laura put her thigh between Chana's and felt the softness of the skin that pressed her own. She felt the moisture of Chana's cunt and the beam of heat that burned out from her. She held still because the feeling inside her was already so full and she just wanted to feel it. A deep satisfaction with the awakening of all her senses, her cells. She breathed in the sweet odor of Chana's neck, squeezed her own thighs and felt the heat coming out of herself. She reached to feel Chana's cunt. So nicely risen, soft and full like a bread with good yeast. Her finger slipped on the wetness as she explored. She felt both nervous and exhilarated, like nearing the peak the first time she climbed a new mountain. Would she be lost? Would she be found? Hearing Chana's response, she knew when her touch was right. She slid into Chana's vagina, a close cave, warm and moist and soft as velvet. A home. A mystery. How perfect that vagina felt and how forceful its being. Like the tide they'd felt while lying in the fog. She wanted to look, and did. Pulled away from Chana and ran her fingers up the path between the lips of her vulva and saw how pink she was. "A beautiful pink garden," she murmured. Her own excitement increased with her words. She had rarely before expressed

110

herself this way. It was a way of being active, of putting the feelings outside, between them, instead of tucked up close to her heart in a bundle the other would have to slowly work to penetrate. A garden was a place to grow in, a place of wonder. These caresses were the seeding of a love which might grow between them.

Chana pulled her back to a long body embrace, breast to breast. She held Laura tight around the hips and Laura felt the energy build heat in her belly. She felt the waves of Chana's energy driving her own higher. She felt her heart so full of feeling. This woman was a stranger, yet she knew her. The whole month following their hike back in the East, she'd felt Chana's presence very close beside her. A loving presence like a guardian angel. She'd felt her spirit in that very bed, and ached with wanting to have her physical presence there.

Chana on top, raised herself up. She was radiant. Her eyes were joyous. Laura ran her fingers through her dark hair, which stood up from her hed. Chana kissed Laura's breasts, her belly, as she moved down to Laura's cunt. There she became the explorer, parting Laura's lips and searching the area gently with her fingers, then licking her. Kissing her. Sucking softly. Laura kept her hands in Chana's soft hair to anchor herself as she rocked her pelvis. She felt vulernable with the absence of Chana's chest against her own, with the open air embracing her there instead, but she could feel love in Chana's mouth on her if she allowed herself to feel there between her legs. It was hard for her to allow full attention concentrated on herself when she was not in the process of actively giving. But she talked to herself: Said take it. Let her love you. Let her find her own pleasure in this. Trust. The receiving required more trust for her than the giving. But when she was able to take in the giving, she glowed inside and moved her pelvis in a way that welcomed Chana's loving. She felt very full. She was on the verge of orgasm. She was on the verge of tears. What would it mean to cry in this woman's arms the first time they'd ever made love? She did not come. She did not cry. Chana came back to hold her full length, her lips next to Laura's ear. Spoke in her soft voice, "I want you to come."

111

Laura's lust peaked at this spoken desire. "I'm moved by the way you touch me, the way you kiss me," she said, knowing as she released these words, they would take her past the tears.

"You can feel that . . . and, still come," Chana said with quiet assurance.

"What about you?" Laura asked.

"I'm easy," Chana replied.

Laura felt the jets of adrenalin shooting from her heart to her belly. She felt her desire growing deeper, like a powerful undertow. Growing stronger and hotter as Chana's invitation ran in her mind. She reached down between them and spread both their lips so her clitoris pressed directly into Chana's, and moved against it. Chana whispered sweet words in her ear. Sometimes she couldn't make them out, but she could feel the care in them, the concentration. This was Laura and Chana together. Their histories were in them, all of the love makings of the past, but this now *was them*. Laura whispered Chana's name. She let her mind go. She was her body. She was the fire and the spirit that moved inside her. She rode it. She had been a long time waiting. Then she tripped off the edge and gasped and felt the glow spread inside her, like a sun coming out strong from behind a cloud. She moaned her pleasure. She felt the tenderness of Chana's arms around her. Her breath came quieter as she lay with her gratitude for the way this was possible, for the miracle of this woman, Chana.

Chana proved her ease. She moved with a confident connection to her body. She built, then stopped still for a moment, savoring some place she had reached she did not want to pass. Then she moved again. She was calling Laura's name, she was speaking to her cunt. Laura looked at her face — so full, so fine with desire, it fired her. Then Chana's breath turned to cries, each breath was a cry, each cry had an echo. Each echo touched Laura's heart. She held her. She held her. She was so happy to be holding her.

Novena

1

*A*LL through the years that Aunt Mary Elizabeth sent me novenas I didn't fully understand them or her or who she was to me. She was gaunt. She stood cooking on the coal stove with her back to me, wearing a cardigan sweater. Her shoulder blades were like the hooks on the kitchen wall where the coats hung — blunt prominences. I thought of the scarecrow in the garden, the overseer. Large scapulae without the flesh filled out. This is what I thought of when her Christmas card came addressed to Mr. and Mrs. Brian Maguire and family. Inside the card was a tiny envelope and inside this envelope a small card inscribed with the message: Commencing December 20, 1950 and continuing for the next nine days, fifteen novenas will be said for you at the request of Miss Mary Elizabeth Maguire. How had she decided on fifteen when there were six of us?

2

Mother bought dish towels for our family to give to Aunt Mary Elizabeth for Christmas. I wandered through the gift shop after mass and imagined myself grown up, with my own money, buying her a beautiful blue holy card with a radiant picture of

Mary on it, or perhaps a scapular. A scapular was to be worn under your clothing, against your skin. The problem was to think of Aunt Mary Elizabeth with skin. She seemed to use her body only as a skeleton she traveled with — to church, to the factory, to the cemetery where she visited the dead.

3

She wrote letters all winter that started and ended with: "The roads are so slippery." She described traveling the river road to the factory every day. "The curves are treacherous," she said, "and the snow gets plowed right over the right bank, and it seems like that's where I'll end if the arthritis doesn't get me first."

4

"Are you scared of the dead?" she asked me once. "I mean does the idea that their flesh has gone cold and heavy frighten you?"

"I guess so," I said, our white gloved hands clasped together.

"You needn't be," she said. "Think of the lightness of the spirit without the body."

Was it walking in the cemetery that made me think her teeth had rattled as she spoke?

5

Spring was her time. In June she wrote: "It's not that I wouldn't like to see you but the nerve of my brother to think I would go away on the long weekend when he knows perfectly well that I always visit the dead on Memorial Day."

Then: "Things grow up so bad in the summer. If you come to visit me you might pass right by this place and not know it's here."

I always think of her in spring — the ground still hard and barren, the snow in dribbles on the north side of the hill. I think of holding her hand, climbing between the gravestones toward Granny and the others — Aunt Mary Elizabeth's stillborn sister and my great uncle Jack who plunged over the river bank and required a good deal of prayer since he was drunk.

Once I sat on one of the stones. Mary Elizabeth had wandered over to visit the neighbors' graves and I found a low stone and sat with my dress pulled down over my knees, my black missal in my lap. I wished that I had one with gold pages. I closed my eyes and tried to communicate to Aunt Mary Elizabeth with my will: Next year for Easter please notice that I don't have a missal with gold-edged pages. Mine have red edges. I opened my eyes again and stared at the sharp contrast of the black book and the white gloves, so pure. She came from behind and pinched my rear just below my waist. She had bumpy joints in her fingers from the arthritis and I couldn't believe she could pinch that hard. I started to yelp but her teeth were in my ear, rattling. "Hush," she said in a whisper. "You were sitting on someone's spirit. How would you like someone to sit on yours?"

A large cloud moved in and I was shivering by the time we reached the car.

7

At home I had a section of my top drawer marked off for Aunt Mary Elizabeth's gifts: Granny's funeral card, a scapular, a white lace mantilla, my blue rosary, some holy cards which I alternated so a different one was showing, my missal, my white gloves. I was a lover of baseball and carried my baseball cards with me. Each time I changed my underwear I had a glance at my Easter gifts, and I knew they were mine, though I was not sure who I was that had them.

8

"Do you still have the rosary I gave you last Easter?"

"Yes, Aunt Mary Elizabeth, the blue one."

"You are a good child to hold onto your things."

She told me my cousin lost hers. "She puts it in her lap and when she kneels it drops and her mind is so much on God that she doesn't hear." Aunt Mary Elizabeth said she told Coleen, "The rosary is a circle, never finished. You can always say another one." She is really telling this to me. "Still I see her rushing," she says of Coleen. "You would think she was going somewhere."

I always thought that Aunt Mary Elizabeth would will all of

Granny's religious objects to this cousin, the first female heir in my generation, but then I saw that I might have a chance if I didn't lose my rosary, if I learned to keep going around the circle without boredom.

9

I lost my religion the year I went away to college but continued to receive my novenas from Aunt Mary Elizabeth in with the family package at Christmas. By the time I was an adult with my own money and could have bought her holy cards, I had forgotten I ever intended to. I had my own apartment, my own dresser. In the top drawer, my missal sat under the last pair of white gloves she had given me. Never worn. She who refused to betray the dead for a Memorial Day weekend away could not be told that I no longer went to church. No longer wore my white gloves, carried my black missal.

But Christmas, a card addressed to me — Miss Irene Maguire — and inside the card, a tiny envelope, and inside that — fifteen novenas. For me, alone. Scarecrow. Overseer. She knew. A woman of vision.

10

"I wish I could travel to visit you but I don't know when," she wrote. "I go down the river road and back six days a week and the factory is always there. They own you in this life but they won't have me in the next.

"At last the roads are not so slippery so I hope you'll come for Easter."

11

Winter was hard here, much freezing rain and the pipes froze more than once, but now I have a warm sun on my back and cool brown earth at my feet. I rake the soil that has just been tilled for the garden. My hands are thin-skinned from winter. Blisters begin to form and the muscles of my back feel as if they are curling into a rope, but the evenness of the patch of ground I have finished draws me to go on.

12

Her brothers always say that Aunt Mary Elizabeth is a

spinster because they did such a fine job of protecting her from their not-to-be-trusted contemporaries when she was young. I wonder what Granny told her. In my memory Granny is an old woman with pure white hair, wrinkles so deep they enfold my imagination. She rocks in a high-backed wicker rocker. She has false teeth, and as I hover around her chair she takes them out, covers their entire mass with her hands and rattles them in my ears. I tell her this gives me goosebumps and she chuckles at my fears.

When Granny died, my mother and father decided I was too young to go to the funeral. How could I explain to them that I thought she meant to invite me?

13

The winter coats still hang in the hall, heavy gloves poking from their pockets. I must cover my hands to go on raking. I am over a decade past childhood and still, in my top drawer, I have a section for relics. And in all these years since Aunt Mary Elizabeth gave me my last pair of white gloves, they have never been worn.

14

The gloves are soft, inside and out, and soothing to my blisters. It is Easter Sunday. I rake my garden until the whole patch has constancy. The gloves are perfect. I am lightheaded with the discovery of them. I furrow several rows for early planting, stoop and drop the seeds with careful spacing. I go back and cover the seeds with a small hill of dirt, tamp it with my gloved hands. I send a message to Aunt Mary Elizabeth: These rows are my novenas for you. I hope that the sun is shining in Pennsylvania where I know Aunt Mary Elizabeth must be visiting Granny in the graveyard.

15

My gloves are still pure white on the back side but have turned brown on the palm side. I remember her pinch: so sudden, so firm. I go on tamping the earth, feeling the rope muscles of my back touched by the sun.

Maureen Brady has been the recipient of a New York State Council on the Arts Writer-in-Residence grant as well as of a CAPS grant. Her published works include two novels: *Folly* and *Give Me Your Good Ear*, stories, plays and articles. Her play, "The True Story of the Elephant in the Living Room," has been produced at the Northampton Center for the Arts in Massachusetts, The WOW Cafe in New York, and will be produced by Bonnie Gable for a national tour in 1987.

She divides her time between New York City and a one room schoolhouse, which is her residence in West Hurley, N.Y.